FROM THE
NANCY DREW FILES

THE CASE: Nancy pursues a counterfeiter who's raised the stakes . . . to murder.

CONTACT: The money was burning a hole in Bess's pocket—but she had no idea how hot it really was.

SUSPECTS: Pamela Carrera— With her modest salary and very expensive wardrobe, the magazine's art director may well be dressed to kill.

Marco Diani—In college, the graphic artist made funny money as a lark . . . but now it's turned into a deadly serious business.

Stuart Teal—He's a smooth operator with charm to spare, but his manner may be as counterfeit as his bankroll.

COMPLICATIONS: Nancy's discovering just how irresistible Stuart Teal can be . . . even though she could be flirting with danger.

Books in The Nancy Drew Files® Series

Available from ARCHWAY Paperbacks

The NANCY DREW Files™
102

COUNTERFEIT CHRISTMAS

CAROLYN KEENE

AN ARCHWAY PAPERBACK
Published by POCKET BOOKS
New York London Toronto Sydney Tokyo Singapore

AN ARCHWAY PAPERBACK *Original*

An Archway Paperback published by
POCKET BOOKS, a division of Simon & Schuster Inc.
1230 Avenue of the Americas, New York, NY 10020

ISBN: 0-671-88193-0

First Archway Paperback printing December 1994

10 9 8 7 6 5 4 3 2 1

NANCY DREW, AN ARCHWAY PAPERBACK and colophon
are registered trademarks of Simon & Schuster Inc.

THE NANCY DREW FILES is a trademark of
Simon & Schuster Inc.

Cover art by Cliff Miller

Printed in the U.S.A.

IL 6+

Chapter

One

"A MILLION DOLLARS! What could I possibly do with a million dollars?" Nancy Drew joked, feigning innocence and shrugging her shoulders.

"You'd find *something* to spend it on," Bess Marvin teased.

"Come on, Nan, fantasize a little," George Fayne urged as she gestured around the River Heights Mall. "A trip around the world, a warehouse full of designer clothes . . . You must want something!"

Nancy could tell that her two closest friends were really into the idea of their being teenage millionaires. "Give me some time to think about this. I'll tell you later," Nancy answered, playing along.

1

Slowly she surveyed her surroundings and took in the tiny gold lights glinting in every store window and the twin glass elevators decked in red and green bows. A banner hung from the second floor balcony, declaring ONLY SEVEN MORE SHOPPING DAYS TILL XMAS!

Nancy hoped she could finish the final and most difficult part of her Christmas shopping in that much time: finding a present for her boyfriend, Ned Nickerson. They had a date to exchange gifts on Christmas Eve, when Ned would be home from Emerson College.

The longer she waited, the more confused Nancy became about what to get Ned.

"How about a new computer thing or a stereo or a VCR or a cordless phone!" Bess suggested excitedly.

"I like your ideas, Bess," Nancy said, "but I just don't have the money. Maybe that's what I'd do with my million dollars—buy all of you presents."

The three strode past the food court and twenty-foot Christmas tree out into the open mall. "Do you mind if we stop at the Hip Hop Shop?" Bess asked pleadingly.

"If you don't buy something soon, your aunt Celeste's money will burn a hole in your pocket!" Nancy answered.

A line of customers was streaming into the tiny shop, and Nancy, George, and Bess followed.

Costume jewelry covered every surface. As the girls began browsing, Bess started to grumble. "The sign said they were having a sensational sale," Bess complained. "These prices don't look so sensational to me." She scowled at a pair of faux-pearl earrings with a price of seventy-five dollars.

"Oh, here's something pretty and a lot cheaper," she said, holding up a pair. "What do you think of these? With a red top and black velvet miniskirt?" she asked eagerly.

"On a scale of one to ten, I'd give them an eleven!" Nancy said.

Bess smiled and headed for the cashier. The man rang up the earrings. "Thirty-six seventy-five," he announced. "Will that be cash or charge?"

"Cash," replied Bess, handing two crisp-looking twenty-dollar bills to the young man.

Instead of placing the bills in the register drawer, the cashier scrutinized Bess before speaking. "You're going to have to see the manager," he said, the corners of his mouth turning down.

"I—I don't understand." Bess was confused. The music in the store was so loud that she had to shout to be heard.

3

"Follow me," he said gruffly.

"We're coming with you," Nancy said to Bess.

The cashier navigated the girls through the store to a tiny office at the back. Behind a door marked Manager was a large, bearded man seated at a rickety desk. The cashier handed him something and pointed at Bess. The manager swiveled around to face the wall. Then he turned back and glared at the girls. "What's the trouble?" Nancy asked, squaring her shoulders as she spoke.

"As if you don't already know!" the manager growled.

"We have no idea," Nancy said simply. Bess shifted nervously from foot to foot.

The manager opened his fist to reveal Bess's money. "You may have thought we'd mistake this for cold, hard cash," he spat out, "but you were wrong. I know funny money when I see it, and these twenties are obviously counterfeit!" Holding one of the bills at either end, he snapped it briskly. The girls watched as the twenty-dollar bill ripped in two with an awful tearing sound. The angry man pointed his finger at Bess. "You're staying put until the police get here!" he ordered.

It was only ten minutes before a tall, lean officer appeared at the door, though it felt to

Nancy like several hours. She'd counted on an afternoon of shopping, not on being treated like a criminal!

"That was fast," the store manager said grudgingly, not bothering to introduce himself.

"Officer Shaw," the man said, nodding his head slightly. "The mall's my beat this time of year," he explained, "so I was already up on the second floor. Now, can you give me a rundown on why these young women are here." He slipped a notepad and pen from his back pocket and got ready to write.

Nancy, George, and Bess took turns explaining that Bess was innocent. Bess would still have to go down to the station, the officer insisted. After he'd taken all the information from the store manager, Officer Shaw led Bess to his squad car, suggesting that Nancy and George follow in their car. Nancy was relieved to climb into the blue Mustang after the intense hour they'd just spent.

The mood in the station house was festive. A hearty spruce sat in the lobby, and a pair of off-duty officers were busily setting out food for what looked like the precinct's Christmas party. Nancy gazed longingly at the enormous tray of lasagna as it was placed on a hotplate. Glancing at her watch, she realized it was two o'clock. Of course she was hungry—it had been five hours since she'd eaten.

Once inside Officer Shaw's cubicle, the girls repeated the story of how Bess came to have the counterfeit money. Bess was worried as she spoke. The money had definitely come from her aunt Celeste, and Bess was sure that her aunt had no idea the bills were fake.

As the questioning continued, Nancy couldn't help wondering whether Officer Shaw believed Bess was innocent—his face revealed nothing. It sure is different being on the other side of an investigation, Nancy decided as the man worked on his forms.

Finally the girls were excused and filed out of the stuffy cubicle. Nancy immediately spotted a familiar face. "Chief McGinnis!" she called out, "we—"

The police chief held up his hand. "I've heard all about it," he informed her. "Come along to my office and we'll have a chat." George and Bess headed for the lobby to wait for their friend.

Alone with the police chief, Nancy relaxed almost immediately. After all, hadn't the chief of police known her to solve many mysteries? Surely he'd believe her when she told him Bess's side of the incident.

When Nancy had finished talking, the chief

nodded his head. "Don't be concerned," he assured her. "Your friend Bess is off the hook. We know she's not responsible for making counterfeit money, but we would like to know who is!"

"Tell me more," Nancy asked, intrigued by the idea of creating fake cash.

"Well," the older man began, his voice taking on a confidential tone, "we've had about four reports of fake bills so far. But that's not unusual for this time of year," he added hastily.

"You mean people try to pass fake money at Christmastime?" Nancy marveled.

"Exactly," Chief McGinnis responded. "These particular bills were made on a copy machine—a *very sophisticated* copy machine. Expensive to buy or lease. We call people who copy money 'casual counterfeiters.' So far casual counterfeiting hasn't been a big problem in this part of the country. But I've alerted the Secret Service nonetheless. If we weren't so busy around here handling burglaries and beefing up security right now, I'd pay more attention to our counterfeiters. They're using a color copier—at least for now. That's the only thing we can be sure of."

"What kind of counterfeiters are there besides 'casual' ones?" Nancy inquired.

"Pros, who will use an offset printing press and paper closer to the real thing. Bess's bill ripped in half because the paper was of poor quality. Real currency paper is made of cotton, which is superstrong." Chief McGinnis reached into his wallet and drew out a ten-dollar bill. He snapped it as the store manager had. This time the bill snapped right back. He replaced it in his billfold.

"But you never know with counterfeiters," he added. "They may have used a copier this time, but that doesn't mean they won't get more professional next time. All it takes is a little ingenuity and a lot of greed."

Nancy nodded. "How did the cashier know the money was fake?" Nancy asked. He had only held the bill for a few seconds before exploding at Bess.

"Store owners know there's more fake cash in circulation during the Christmas season. They train their employees. This time the cashier knew the bill felt wrong—the paper was too smooth."

Nancy nodded. "I understand you're swamped right now, Chief," she told him, "so how about if I do a little investigating on my own?"

The police chief's brow furrowed. "Hold off for now, Nancy, but if the picture gets worse, I'll consider it."

"Right, Chief," Nancy responded. She had the feeling McGinnis would be getting back to her before the holidays were over.

* * *

"That's about as much excitement as I can take before a trip," Bess said when they were back in the car. That evening she'd be on her way to California to see Kyle, a former boyfriend, who had been studying so hard in law school that he'd barely had a social life. "It ought to be *illegal* to miss someone so much," he'd written in one of his letters. Eager to know if the relationship had a future, Bess couldn't resist his invitation to visit.

Nancy drove Bess home and hugged her friend goodbye.

"Say hi to Kyle for us," George told her cousin, "and call us if anything juicy happens! We want to be the first to know if you guys get back together."

With any luck, thought Nancy, the counterfeiter would be caught by the time Bess returned on Christmas Eve.

The next afternoon Nancy and George were eating BLT's in Nancy's kitchen when the phone rang.

"Hi, Chief," Nancy said, hoping his call could be the green light for her to start.

"Our problem seems to be spreading," McGinnis reported. "Officer Golubev just turned up five more bills. So if you want to look into this thing—informally, of course—go ahead."

"Great!" said Nancy.

"Here's what to look for," McGinnis instructed. "Counterfeiters must have access to the tools of the trade—color copiers, printing presses, paper. And after they create their fake money, they want to spend it, especially at this time of year. So watch for people who are suddenly spending large amounts of money or living beyond their means."

"Got it," Nancy said. "I'll let you know what I come up with," she promised.

"Excellent," McGinnis told her. "Just one more thing: Be careful—counterfeiting is a dirty business!"

The headquarters of *River Heights Magazine* was the best place to start, Nancy reasoned. After all, the fake bills had come from Bess's aunt, who was the advertising director for *River Heights Magazine*.

Nancy and George found Celeste Goodman easily. Nancy judged Celeste to be in her midforties, slim, attractive, but visibly tense. When Nancy explained the purpose of her visit, Celeste grew even edgier.

"Oh, my, poor Bess! I had no idea about the m—money," she stammered. "I can assure you that Bess is innocent, and for that matter so am I.

If only I could help point you to the real counterfeiter!"

All at once a figure appeared in the doorway. "Is someone looking for a counterfeiter?" a male voice boomed. "Well, look no further! I can tell you who it is!"

Chapter

Two

YOU MEAN YOU KNOW who's been passing fake money?" Celeste asked anxiously. Nancy and George were both puzzled.

"Of course, I thought everybody knew," the man replied casually. "Didn't you know that Pamela in the art department has been printing fake cash since Thanksgiving? Where do you think our Christmas bonuses are coming from!"

Celeste chuckled. "Nancy Drew and George Fayne, meet Jason Greene, our resident business writer—and *comedian*. I can assure you that Jason's really very serious. Here, let me show you." She leafed through an issue of the magazine to find a two-page article about the stock market with the byline By Jason Greene.

"You must know quite a bit about money," Nancy commented. "Tell us more about this counterfeiter in your art department."

"Maybe we could even see the operation and meet the ringleader," George kidded. "I don't think I've ever met a real counterfeiter before."

"We'll definitely take a tour of the art department before you leave," Jason said. "Seriously, what is all this I hear about fake cash?" Jason asked, seating himself next to Nancy.

"Apparently, someone around town has been making and using counterfeit bills," Celeste said, her voice trembling slightly. "Nancy and George have traced a couple of the bills to me."

"Do you happen to recall who might have given you the money that you gave Bess for Christmas?" Nancy asked the older woman.

"I know precisely where the money came from," Celeste replied with conviction. "From one of the kids who went skiing with us last month," she began.

"Celeste is mother hen around here," Jason explained to the girls. "She makes sure all the employees get plenty of rest and relaxation."

Pressing her fingers to her temples, Celeste continued, "Most of the deposit money for the ski trip—two hundred dollars per person—was paid by check. But a couple of people did pay in cash. . . ."

"Who were they?" Nancy asked. It would be lucky if they could narrow down the suspects to a few people.

Celeste paused. "I'm not sure I really remember." She chewed distractedly on her thumbnail.

"Is there a record of the payments?" George prompted.

"Of course," said Celeste. "I have a list—if only I can find it . . ." Her voice trailed off. Nancy made a mental note of how flustered Celeste was acting.

"Take your time," Nancy suggested. Celeste, after all, was a friend of Bess's family. Bess had called the woman "aunt" since childhood. Nancy didn't want to make the investigation any harder for Celeste than it had to be.

As Celeste searched for her list, Nancy had a chance to scrutinize Jason. He certainly was good-looking, she noted, trying to stay objective. He was in his late twenties, she judged, and well over six feet tall, maybe six three. With straight dirty-blond hair and clear blue eyes, he resembled a California surfer in a business suit!

"I've got it," Celeste announced moments later, holding up a sheaf of papers. She adjusted her bifocals and ran her finger down a column of names. "The people who paid the deposit in cash are Pamela Carrera and Chloe Lee!" She sounded surprised. "I don't understand. Pamela's the art director here—very professional. What would she be doing with fake money?" Celeste spoke in a rush, her thoughts obviously racing. "And I've known Chloe Lee since she started as a contributor here. She's one of our best talents. I'm sure she had no idea the money wasn't real."

"I agree," Jason said, reaching over and taking the pad from Celeste's hands. "Chloe must've gotten the money from someone else," Jason insisted.

"Chloe's a cartoonist. She's young but already successful. She *has* money, so she wouldn't need to manufacture it." Celeste pointed to some illustrations on the bulletin board. "Her Penny the Dog comic strip started right here at the magazine."

"I knew her name sounded familiar," Nancy remarked. She smiled at the stylized drawings of the English bull terrier.

"And I think you should know," Jason said, a touch self-consciously, "that Chloe is my girl-friend. We've been going out for six months now."

Celeste continued, "Jason was our most eligible bachelor—until I introduced him to Chloe."

"And I'm more than grateful to Celeste for

that," Jason confided. "By the way," he added, "Chloe's up for the Illinois Society of Cartoonists Gold Medal."

"Fabulous!" Celeste responded. Celeste took a step toward Nancy and placed a hand on her shoulder. "There's something else I can tell you," Celeste continued earnestly. "As soon as you meet her, you'll know for yourself that Chloe Lee isn't capable of wrongdoing. Heaven only knows how she may have ended up with counterfeit money!"

"How about that tour of the art department?" George asked Jason once the three young people had left Celeste's office.

"Right this way," Jason answered. He came to a stop after passing several offices with closed doors.

Jason pointed to an office, apparently belonging to Pamela. It was behind an enormous plate-glass window; there was no one sitting at the desk. "No one home. She ought to be back soon. Pamela's department is putting the latest issue to bed," he informed Nancy and George. "So she could be here half the night making last-minute changes. And you can't miss her—she's got flaming red hair down to her waist."

Nancy nodded and then told Jason they were ready to leave. In the corridor outside the art department, she turned to him. "Thanks for giving us the lay of the land," she said. Perhaps later that evening she and George would be able to catch Pamela. Jason did say she'd work half the night. After all, Pamela and Chloe are our only leads so far, Nancy thought.

Jason offered to take the girls to meet Chloe at her studio. "It's only a fifteen-minute drive," he explained, "and I'm on my way over after work to help out with a computer snafu."

Nancy and George accepted the offer. "How about we take my car?" Jason suggested. "It's new, and I have a feeling you girls will get a kick out of it." He tossed her the keys. "Go ahead and I'll be with you in a sec. I just want to call Chloe and let her know we're coming. It's the black Jeep parked right next to the front entrance."

Inside the car, Nancy was grateful for the few minutes of privacy.

"It was nice of Jason to take us to meet Chloe," George commented. "I don't think we'll get anything but praise from him or Celeste. They're not just Chloe's friends, they're her official fan club."

"You're right." Nancy nodded. "We'll just have to . . ." She broke off and waved to Jason.

The young man strode up to the car and slid into the front seat. "Onward ho!" he intoned, starting the engine and putting the car into gear.

"Too bad it's five below," Jason said, "otherwise I'd put the top down." Nancy shivered at the thought of the winter wind in her hair at fifty-five miles an hour.

The ride was bouncy, but Nancy and George loved it. "What a neat Jeep this is!" George said appreciatively as they zoomed along the highway.

"I got a great deal," Jason offered. "The guy who owned it before me needed to sell it in a hurry. Otherwise I'd never have been able to afford it," he said. "Now Pamela, on the other hand," he said, "always has money. I don't know where she gets it, but she sure knows how to spend it! You should see *her* car."

I will see it, Nancy thought, just as soon as I get a chance.

Jason maneuvered the vehicle up the driveway of a rectangular redbrick building that was obviously a converted warehouse. "This is it," he announced, as proudly as if he'd built the place himself.

The studio was more like a playroom than an office. It was one large, open space plus an enclosed conference room and a balcony. The walls were papered with comic strips all bearing Chloe's signature.

"Hi—and welcome!" a voice rang out. For a moment Nancy couldn't determine from where the greeting came. But soon she adjusted her vision to the balcony, where a petite woman waved enthusiastically. Her straight jet black hair reached just to her shoulders. She wore a red jumpsuit with a black belt and black boots. Chloe Lee was a knockout.

Chloe glided down the steps and walked over to meet the two girls. "You must be Nancy Drew and George Fayne here to see me about the counterfeit money," she said quickly. She turned and murmured hello to Jason, kissing him lightly on the cheek.

"Come on in and look around," Chloe invited. "Jason, could you look at the big-screen computer as well as the one on the balcony? The monitor's been on the blink and I won't get a chance to fix it. I'll be in the conference room with Nancy and George."

Jason seemed eager to help. "I'll check it out and catch up with you later. Since it's getting late, maybe we can grab some early dinner at Creative Planet when you're through," he replied, mounting the stairs.

"Sounds great to me," Chloe answered. "I'll try to talk these guys into it."

When the three young women were seated at the conference table, Nancy said to Chloe, "We're glad you could see us on such short notice. We're trying to find out how you could have gotten counterfeit twenty-dollar bills, if they were from you."

When Chloe answered, she sounded sincere but sad. "I wish I could tell you. I paid Celeste that deposit almost two months ago. I couldn't possibly remember where the money came from. I'm afraid I could've gotten the money any-place!" Nancy nodded as Chloe spoke.

"And I tend to focus on the creative side of my business rather than the financial details," Chloe continued. "So I wouldn't be likely to remem-ber."

"I understand," Nancy said sympathetically. Suddenly a man appeared at the door. Nancy fixed her gaze on the slender young fellow.

Chloe turned to see who was there. "Marco!" said the cartoonist. "Why didn't you tell me you were here?" Chloe became uncomfortable. With-out waiting for him to answer, she introduced the bashful young man. "Marco Diani, meet Nancy Drew and George Fayne. Marco and I share this studio space. He's the most talented graphic designer in River Heights," Chloe claimed. She was talking fast now. Marco couldn't have gotten a word in if he'd wanted to, Nancy observed.

Marco was handsome with wavy black hair and olive skin. He was younger than Jason or Chloe and far less sure of himself. Marco was strangely quiet, like a mime, gesturing instead of speaking.

"He designs posters, ads, brochures. I'm sure you've seen his stuff around town," Chloe was saying.

Apparently too shy or frightened to speak in front of Nancy and George, Marco bent to whisper in Chloe's ear.

"You don't have to whisper," she said. "Of course you can use my colored pencils. We're thinking of going over to Creative Planet for some dinner. Come with us, Marco—you've got to eat. I'll bet you'll even enjoy yourself."

Chloe acts more like his mother than his partner, Nancy thought. What's going on here?

"If you insist, then I will come," he said in a low tone. Nancy heard a strong Italian accent. "But please, Chloe, can you come with me now just for one moment?" He was pleading with her.

"Excuse me just a sec," Chloe said, disappearing through the door and closing it behind her.

Nancy turned to George and said, "I'll be right back, too—just going for a quick tour!" George gave Nancy a thumbs-up.

Nancy darted out of the conference room and past a desk. In an alcove she noticed a pair of louvered doors that probably concealed a closet. Yanking open the doors, Nancy hesitated as she took in the array of machines and equipment.

She swiftly identified a slide projector, several portfolio cases of various sizes, plus a stereo and a CD player. Expensive stuff, Nancy thought, but nothing particularly suspicious.

Just then she noticed a narrow space on the side of the equipment—just enough room for a person to slip by. Could there be another layer of machines behind the first one? It was difficult to see all the way back since she had only the light from the main room.

Nancy eased past the portfolio cases, searching for what they concealed. Her hunch was right: The closet was deep—deep enough to hold twice as much! A large, square object came into view. It was waist high and created a steady whirring sound. Nancy examined the control panel.

Playing a hunch, Nancy removed her driver's license from her handbag. She lifted the top flap of the machine, placed her license facedown, and pushed the button. After a full minute, the machine spit out a sheet of paper. There was an exact replica of her license, including the color photo. Someone in the studio had a fancy color copier, just like the one Chief McGinnis had described!

Chapter

Three

NANCY FROZE, ideas whizzing through her head. Could Chloe have used this machine to run off the fake twenties? Who else in the office had access to this machine? And why was it concealed behind closed doors?

Nancy folded the color copy and slid it into her pocket. This is a sophisticated machine, she noted, examining the control panel of more than fifteen buttons.

Hearing the tapping of Chloe's heels against the wooden floor, Nancy quickly found her way back to the front of the closet and eased the doors shut behind her. She coughed loudly to cover the squeak of the louvered doors' wheels. Nancy slipped into the conference room, thankful that

Chloe's conversation with Marco had taken a few minutes.

A moment later Chloe bounced into the room with Jason. "Okay," she said cheerily. "It may be early, but I'm declaring it dinnertime! Jason, Nancy, and George are going to join us at Creative Planet."

Jason acted dismayed for a quick moment, so Chloe quickly reached over and touched his arm. "Why don't you call Stuart and see if he can come also," she said. "I'm sure the girls would enjoy meeting someone who runs a printing company, since they're on the trail of counterfeiters. Stuart Teal runs the business for his family. He's a good friend of ours."

Jason shifted to face Marco and said, "Well, then, you've got to join us as well, Marco."

Marco searched Chloe's face for an answer. He mumbled something about a deadline, but Jason cut him off by saying, "It's just a quick dinner, and you have to eat if you're going to be working."

"Okay, then it's all settled. Let's get ready," Chloe declared.

One thing's for sure, Nancy thought, if this woman's in the business of counterfeiting, she does it with confidence!

* * *

Nancy had heard of but never been to Creative Planet. World globes of every size and description hung from the ceiling of the room. The walls were covered with drawings and illustrations.

Stuart Teal greeted Jason at the door. "Hey, pal," Jason responded, clapping his friend on the back.

After the introductions were made, Nancy had a few moments to check out Stuart Teal. He was shorter than Jason by at least two inches but still more than six feet tall. His brown eyes matched his straight chestnut hair. Stuart appeared to be in his late twenties and equally as successful as Jason. His navy blue double-breasted suit fit beautifully, Nancy noticed, and he had all the right touches: leather-trimmed suspenders, gold cuff links and matching tie clip, plus shiny black wing-tipped shoes.

Stuart pulled out Nancy's chair for her when they reached the table. He sat beside her and swiftly opened a menu and placed it in her hands.

"Thank you, Stuart," Nancy said politely, wondering if he always paid so much attention to people.

Creative Planet was known for its burgers, so everyone ordered the specialty along with colas and french fries.

When the food arrived, Stuart tossed his silk designer necktie over his shoulder. "I don't want to end up wearing my dinner," he said to Nancy with a grin.

George whispered to Nancy when everyone was busy, "They're adorable, Nan."

Nancy nodded, sipping her soda.

Halfway through the meal, Jason cleared his throat. "You know, Nancy and George, I asked Stuart to come along because I thought he'd be helpful in the matter at hand. Stuart's president of Perfect Printing. He knows quite a bit about the printing business—and everything else."

"That's lucky," George said.

"Mmmm-hmmm," agreed Nancy. "Maybe you could fill us in on printing techniques," she suggested to Stuart. Had Jason assumed the fake money was printed on a regular press and not a color copier? Nancy wondered. Or was he just playing dumb?

"But, of course," Stuart said smoothly, giving Nancy a long look. "Why not come by the plant tomorrow, say, first thing—nine A.M. I'd be happy to show you the ropes."

Her heart skipped a beat despite her effort to remain cool. There was no mistaking the signal that Stuart was intrigued by Nancy and that he was available.

A deep flush colored Nancy's face. She cleared her throat and turned to Marco to include him in the conversation. "Marco," she asked softly, "where in Italy are you from?"

"Milano—I mean Milan. My family moved there from Rome when I was three years old." He blinked anxiously.

"How interesting! How long have you been living in the States?"

"For several years," he told her shyly, offering no more information.

"We all went to school together, Chloe, Jason, Marco, and I," Stuart explained. "We were at Wrenton High School for four years—all four of us, even though the boy-genius, Marco, is younger."

"Then Marco and I went to the Chicago School of Design," Chloe said.

"And Stu and I went on to become rich and famous!" Jason teased.

Jason gestured toward Marco. "You should have seen this guy when he first came to this country," he interjected. "He was only fifteen and could hardly speak English."

"But isn't it amazing how fast he learned?" Chloe said hurriedly, trying to soften the impact of Jason's harsh words.

Marco looked up from his food, which he'd

hardly touched. He cleared his throat as if about to speak, but he remained silent.

"Tell you what," Jason offered, breaking the tension. "How would you all like to come to the cartoonist society's dinner on Wednesday night?" he asked. "I reserved a whole table, exactly six places. I'm sure you'll have a great time," he urged. "What d'you say?"

"Sounds like fun," Nancy admitted.

"It's all right with me," George responded. "What's the dress?"

"Black tie, of course," Jason answered.

George groaned.

"She's happier in cleats and sweats," Nancy explained, and everyone laughed.

The waitress arrived with the bill and diplomatically placed it in the middle of the table. Each of the men reached for his wallet; each woman gathered her handbag. Chloe placed her purse in Jason's hands, asking him to pay for her while she visited the ladies' room.

Somehow, the mood was tense. Jason quickly calculated the amount each person owed. He drew two fives from his wallet. As he placed them on the table he grinned, joking, "Gee, I sure hope none of this is counterfeit!"

Nancy chuckled politely with the others.

Stuart offered Nancy and George a ride back to

their car. After promising to meet for a tour of Perfect Printing the next morning, the girls climbed into Nancy's Mustang.

"Now," George said matter-of-factly, "what did you see at the studio?"

As Nancy described the elaborate copier in the closet, George nodded, and Nancy knew they were thinking the same thing.

"We've got to go back," Nancy said. "We need to look around without anyone else there."

"How about soon—like now!" George suggested. Nancy turned the car around and headed toward the warehouse.

"Item number two, Stuart Teal!" George began. "He's totally cute and thinks you're beautiful. I think it's called love at first sight!"

Nancy winced. "I'll admit he was paying tons of attention to me, but I wouldn't exactly call it love—"

"What I'd like to know is, what Ned's going to say when he gets back from school?" George teased.

The girls were roughly a quarter of a mile from the studio. "We'd better stop here," Nancy said, easing the Mustang onto the shoulder. She parked and removed a powerful flashlight and other paraphernalia from the glove compartment.

The girls walked the remaining five hundred yards in silence. The dark warehouse loomed before them at the top of a small ridge. They took long strides up the incline and circled around to the side of the building.

Nancy stopped short, gripping George's arm to keep her from advancing. "Wait," Nancy rasped. A dim light shone through a small basement window right beside them. Voices could be heard coming from it.

Nancy and George darted beside the window, crouching low against the building.

The voices grew louder, and Nancy could make out one male voice and one female.

"I'm sick of him!" a male voice exclaimed. "And I'm sick of being a designer!"

"Listen," the female coaxed, "I know you're upset, but you're just jealous—"

"What am I jealous of?" the voice demanded.

"It's Marco," Nancy whispered.

"You envy Jason," the woman answered, adding, "but you've got to try not to. Things with me and Jason just aren't going to change: I'm in love with him. You've got to accept that."

"He's a monster," Marco accused. "He treats me like a little brother or pet animal!" The designer's voice was plaintive now.

"I'm sorry, really I am," Chloe responded. "And I've asked him not to do it. But Jason's just that way. Please, Marco, get used to it so we can go through with our plans."

Nancy and George held their breath as they waited for the argument to unfold.

"If that is the way you feel," Marco said forcefully, "then I assure you there'll be some changes in our deal."

Chapter

Four

NANCY AND GEORGE WAITED a few minutes in the subzero night after Marco went outside before walking back to their car. With Chloe still in the building, they'd have to postpone checking it out until the following day. Only in the privacy of Nancy's car could they wonder aloud at what Marco and Chloe had been talking about and what they were doing in the basement.

"I know we've got to investigate Pamela, but it sure is scary here at night," George whispered to Nancy as they stood peering at the *River Heights Magazine* building. Its front columns cast long shadows against the entrance walkway.

"Let's get in and out fast," Nancy suggested,

rubbing her hands together in an effort to stay warm.

"Right," affirmed George. She then pressed the illuminated night bell to the right of the building's glass doors.

The security guard raised his eyes from the paperback he was reading, set the book aside, and strode to meet them.

"What in heaven's name brings you out on a frigid night like this!" the man said in an amazed but friendly manner.

"Duty calls," George responded. "We have to see Pamela Carrera." It was the fib Nancy and George had agreed upon in the car; they hoped the guard would let them pass without asking too many questions.

"Hold on just a minute," he said affably. "Let me ring her for you. Meanwhile, sign the security register." The man handed George a clipboard and pen, then dialed the house phone and paused. "She's not at her desk," he reported a moment later, "but she can't have gone far. You girls look innocent enough; go on back."

"Thanks," Nancy called out as she and George scooted down the hall toward Pamela's office.

They saw a woman with waist-length red hair conversing with a young man. She was wearing a finely cut rust-colored suit with lavishly embroidered lapels. The art director's nails were pol-

33

ished a shade that perfectly coordinated with the suit. Her black suede shoes looked brand-new and expensive.

"Who are *you?*" she demanded when she'd finished her conversation.

Nancy and George told Pamela the reason for their visit.

"What kind of investigation are we talking about here?" she said sharply.

"Why don't we talk about it in your office," Nancy said tactfully.

Huffing impatiently, Pamela dismissed her employee and marched into her office. Nancy and George followed, closing the door behind them.

As Nancy elaborated on the purpose of the visit, Pamela's voice grew shrill. "So I'm supposed to tell you how, out of the fifteen zillion possible places in this town, I got my hands on money that you're telling me is counterfeit?" Nancy noticed that Pamela wasn't just angry, there seemed to be panic in her voice.

Nancy kept her tone even. "I know it's tricky, but we'd appreciate it if you could try to recall how you got the bills."

"I don't have time for this—I have a magazine to produce," she said. "But if you *must* have an answer, I'll think about it until tomorrow." Pamela sounded pressured. She was not really willing to cooperate, and Nancy felt there was no choice but to continue the interview at another time.

"Of course." Nancy nodded. "One of us will give you a call tomorrow to see when you're available."

The art director's face relaxed. "I'll have the story—I mean the information for you then." Nancy couldn't help responding to Pamela's slip of the tongue. Did the art director need the extra time to concoct a story? Or was she just stressed out?

"You wouldn't believe how many *stories* I've got to have typeset by tomorrow at noon," Pamela said quickly, obviously trying to cover her mistake.

"No problem," said Nancy as she and George rose to leave. "We'll count on seeing you tomorrow when your deadline is over." Then we'll find out if you're telling the truth, she said to herself.

The next morning, gray clouds hung over the Perfect Printing plant as Nancy's car approached the black wrought-iron gates. A guard at the security station leaned out and waved them in.

"That's funny," Nancy said, pulling into a parking space marked VISITORS. "How does he know it was okay to let us in?"

"Beats me," George said, "but I bet we'll find out."

It was only eight fifty-one, so Nancy suggested they wait until nine to go on in.

"What d'you say, Nan?" George asked. "Are you looking forward to seeing Stuart again?"

"Of course," Nancy answered lightly. "At least he's friendlier than Pamela. I'm not looking forward to seeing her again."

"I'm with you, Nan," George responded.

A strongly built gray-haired woman greeted them as they entered the building. "I'm Yvonne Pollane, Mr. Teal's assistant. Welcome to Perfect Printing," she said warmly. "Security told us you were here. Mr. Teal will be with you in just a few moments."

"Thank you," said Nancy, stifling a yawn. All the action from the day before seemed to be catching up to her.

"It's certainly a dreary, sleepy morning," Yvonne said, smiling and handing them each a cup of coffee.

The people here are nice, Nancy thought. It's almost spooky. They gave her what she wanted before she even knew she wanted it!

Nancy felt her stomach tighten when Stuart walked into the reception area. His step faltered for just a second. They both smiled at the same time. He was just as fashionable as he had been the night before, only this time he wore a gray suit with a yellow silk handkerchief in his breast pocket.

"You look lovely this morning," he said, complimenting Nancy. She was wearing a green fitted merino wool dress with brass-colored buttons and a metallic headband.

"Let's go to my office," he said, guiding them through a set of swinging metal doors. Stuart's office was spacious, with a wine-colored leather sofa and three upholstered chairs in addition to a traditional mahogany desk. Stuart seated himself in his plush desk chair. Leaning back, he stretched his arms behind his head, motioning for Nancy and George to sit on the sofa facing him. After chatting for a few minutes, Nancy steered the conversation toward the purpose of their visit.

"Thanks for offering to show us around," she said. "We're interested in finding out more about printing—how money is printed, in particular."

"Whoa!" Stuart said, straightening up in his chair. "We may use the same machines that counterfeiters do, but that's just a coincidence. We make plenty of money here, but we do it the old-fashioned way: by earning it. We've never been in the business of printing fake cash."

He seems a little defensive, Nancy thought.

"Of course you don't make counterfeit money," Nancy reassured him, "but we are curious about which of the printing techniques are the same."

"Well, then," he said, sounding relieved, "I can tell you a lot about printing. In fact, this is a family business. The Teals have been printers since 1936. But as far as currency is concerned, no *ordinary* printer can tell you how it's done because there are so many steps that are kept secret."

"What do you mean by 'ordinary' printer?" Nancy questioned. If Stuart was an 'ordinary' printer, then what were currency printers called?

"An ordinary shop is one like mine. We print mostly newspapers, some magazines, and little stuff like letterheads for companies.

"But the places that print American money are called security printers. They're the people the government hires to actually print money. You can imagine how much security they need to keep that operation straight."

"I see," said Nancy. "So it's security printers who'd know about counterfeiting."

"I'd think so," Stuart agreed. "And you can find one near here. All you have to do is go to Knightsville, less than an hour away. National Printing Arts is a security printer, and they'll tell you all about the process."

"Are you saying you couldn't print money here even if you wanted to?" George asked.

"Not legally," Stuart answered. "And besides, printing *real* money, the way security printers do it, is really complicated. You need an engraved plate to put on the printing press. You need the right paper, currency paper, and that's something only one supplier can give you. Let's see what else—you'd need special ink. *And* you have to have the right presses. Again, that's to make authentic American currency." For an ordinary printer, Stuart seemed to know an awful lot about printing money, Nancy thought.

"I see," said Nancy. "On Perfect's presses you could only make some forgeries and not the real thing," Nancy ventured, softening her words with a smile.

"Sure, I could turn out some fake bills. But I'd be a fool to try." Stuart's eyes narrowed. "From what I hear, most people who've ever tried counterfeiting get caught sooner or later—and it's usually sooner rather than later!"

Stuart stood up from his desk and announced enthusiastically, "Let the tour begin."

Five gargantuan machines were running at once on the printing room floor. The distinctive sound of rollers crashing together filled the air:

Ker-chin-ka! Ker-chin-ka! came from each machine, creating a crazy rhythm.

Overwhelmed by the din, Nancy and George brought their hands to their ears.

"Try these," Stuart shouted, producing ear plugs from his back pocket and handing them to the girls. Nancy asked if it was okay to check out the first press. Stuart nodded and followed Nancy as she wove through the maze of presses.

Stuart snapped a notebook out of his pocket along with a fancy fountain pen. He scrawled: "This is called a web press. It can print six colors at a time!"

Nancy felt tiny standing next to the long, noisy machine. She watched with fascination as a printer fed a giant roll of white paper into the press. Two other men helped.

Stuart touched Nancy's arm and pointed to a wide yellow strip marked SAFETY LINE painted on the floor. She stepped behind the line but continued to peer at the intricate machine. She saw ink trays distributing ink onto rollers, rollers spinning, and a long blur of color; the process was unfolding so fast it was impossible to tell the colors apart. If posters could be produced this fast, imagine how much money could be printed in an hour! Nancy reasoned.

Nancy and George made their way to the far end of the press. The fellow at that end checked each piece as it shot off the press and into the holding tray. Nancy examined the stacks of newly printed material: vibrant posters advertising an upcoming dance performance.

They passed by a smaller printing press. This one had a single person overseeing a much smaller job; for the moment, she was stationed at the paper feed part of the press. At the other end, corporate letterhead shot out of the machine, pausing momentarily before settling into place in the tray. While Stuart's back was turned, Nancy reached behind her to the reject pile of letterheads that the printers had tossed aside at the beginning of the process. She seized a single piece, folded it quickly, and placed it in her handbag. It might come in handy later, she thought.

As they passed into the next room, the automatic folding machines created their own distinctive sound. *Pocket-a pocket-a* Nancy heard softly through the ear plugs. The noise came from twin folding machines as they spit out small square posters ready to be inserted into the center of a magazine.

Stuart led the girls down a long hallway to a third area, a vast storeroom crammed with cartons. The printer removed his ear plugs, and his visitors followed suit.

"This, as you can see, is the stockroom," he

declared. "Over there," he said, pointing, "the paper and finished product get stored. That's why it's cooler in here—temperature control."

Just then Yvonne stepped into the room. "Telephone call for you, Mr. Teal—long distance. It's the Geissbuhler Company from Switzerland," she said.

"Thank you, Yvonne. I'll call them back in an hour."

"They said it's rather important," she insisted.

"I'll call them back later," he said sternly. It was the first time Nancy had seen Stuart being difficult.

"Yes, sir," she said curtly, turning on her heel and leaving the room.

Switzerland was a world away from River Heights, and the Swiss are well known for their printing skills, Nancy thought. What business could Stuart's firm have with them, and why wasn't he more eager to take the phone call? she wondered.

Stuart led Nancy and George to the loading dock. "This is where we receive all of our deliveries and make all of our shipments," Stuart said matter-of-factly.

The opening to the loading dock was twenty-five feet wide, big enough to accommodate the back of a truck. Long plastic strips hung from the top of the gap, probably to keep the heat inside the building, Nancy surmised.

Stuart, Nancy, and George stepped through the opening to the outside of the building. Nancy found herself standing on a platform. She could see now that there was a back entrance to the plant, a wide paved road branched off the main thoroughfare and led to it.

She spotted a large commercial truck making its way toward the loading dock. When the vehicle was within several yards of the loading dock, it backed up, apparently in preparation for a delivery. Before Nancy knew what was happening, the truck had zoomed toward her in reverse, then stopped abruptly. The doors at the back of the truck were flung open, and she saw that there was a masked person inside—a masked person hurling a huge carton straight at her!

Chapter

Five

STANDING AT THE VERY EDGE of the loading dock, Nancy had nowhere to go but down to avoid the flying carton.

She landed on the asphalt seven feet down on her feet, but the impact caused her to tumble backward. Automatically she thrust her arms behind her, breaking her fall with her hands.

At the same time, the carton landed heavily on the dock above her. George and Stuart had rolled out of the path of the hurtling box.

From below, Nancy watched Stuart scramble to his feet and rush to the edge of the platform. "I'll be right there," he called. "Are you all right!?"

"I'm fine," she responded.

Stuart and George hurried down the loading dock steps and came around to where Nancy sat. Most of the damage was superficial: Her stocking had a noticeable run, and her headband had flown off.

"Are you sure you're not hurt?" Stuart asked, kneeling next to Nancy to examine her.

"That was quite a jump, Nan," George added, arriving behind Stuart.

The printing executive extended his hand to help Nancy up off the ground. Grasping his fingers, she winced and was stopped cold by the shooting pain in her wrist. "Actually," she said, downplaying her injury, "my wrist is a little sore right there. I must have sprained it a bit," she admitted.

"Allow me, then," Stuart announced. Before Nancy could protest, he circled her waist with his arm and whisked her to her feet in a single, strong motion.

When Stuart's arm lingered around her waist for a few seconds longer than necessary, Nancy was pleased at the reassuring touch and disappointed when the moment ended. She had to remind herself she was on a case.

Once they were back inside and seated in Stuart's office, Nancy told Stuart she'd go back to the dock and check the contents of the carton. It could just have been a deliveryman with lousy aim. But why the mask? she had to ask herself, knowing it was no simple mistake.

Nancy asked Stuart not to call the police. She could explain to the chief what she felt he had to know.

The girls walked back to the dock and opened the carton. It was filled with rocks. No accident. When they were finally out of earshot back in the car, Nancy turned to George.

"Someone obviously wants us off this case and doesn't care if we get hurt. I think whoever it is will stop short of killing us because the person could have backed the truck over me."

George nodded solemnly. "But the only people who know we're investigating are Stuart, Chloe, Jason, Marco, Pamela, and Celeste."

"Well, then," Nancy said, "I guess those are our suspects for the moment." She put the car in drive and headed for the *River Heights Magazine* building.

When they arrived at the magazine building, Nancy fluffed up her hair and put on fresh lipstick, using the rearview mirror.

"I can't meet with the art director of *River Heights Magazine* looking rumpled, especially after she gave me such a hard time this morning about scheduling a noon appointment," Nancy declared.

Once inside the building, George waited for Nancy to change into fresh stockings in the ladies' room. Then they proceeded to Pamela's office.

A shade now covered the vast plate-glass window. No light shone out from under the shade or around the edges.

George strode into the art area and Nancy followed. "Have you seen Pamela Carrera today?" George asked a man.

"Yeah," he replied. "She's, um, out to lunch and won't be back until later."

"How long ago did she leave?" George persisted.

"About ten minutes ago," the man guessed.

The art director had known they were coming, and yet she deliberately was out when they arrived. At the very least, Pamela was being evasive.

As if reading Nancy's mind, George whispered, "Let's go." While the young man's back was turned, they slipped into Pamela's office.

Not wanting to arouse suspicion by turning on the light, Nancy pulled a flashlight from her purse. "Let's see if we can come up with whatever it is that Pamela's trying to hide," Nancy said in a low tone as she pulled open Pamela's desk drawers. The top drawer revealed nothing more than a wide-tooth comb, a compact, and paper clips. The files below showed nothing unusual, so Nancy crouched to explore beneath the desk.

George stood by the wooden door, ready to alert Nancy if they were interrupted.

After five minutes Nancy moved to a floor-to-ceiling cabinet set into the wall behind Pamela's desk. Nancy tugged on the door, but it refused to open. Nancy reached into her purse and took out a plastic credit card, which she inserted into the gap between the door and the frame. She whooshed it upward in one swift motion, and the door opened, spilling out an avalanche of bags.

"What's going on?" George whispered furiously.

"Give me a sec," Nancy said, scooping up the contents of the top bag.

A gold lamé blouse glinted up at Nancy. She ran the light over the collection of bags and discovered that each one bore the name of a women's clothing store. "She's got clothes—lots of them—in bags," Nancy said, examining the neck of the blouse. "This one's an Italian designer number, and it cost twelve hundred dollars!"

"Great," replied George. "We've got a clothes horse on our hands. Now all we have to figure out is whether she buys them with her own money, steals them, or prints her own money to be able to afford them!"

"Mmmm-hmmm," Nancy agreed, folding the top and putting it neatly back in the bag. This may be the clue we've been looking for, she decided. Pamela had a whole art department full of tools to support counterfeiting. And she had a cupboard stocked with costly designer clothes— far more than anyone could afford on the salary of a small magazine's art director. Nancy knew it would take more sleuthing to know exactly how far Pamela Carrera would go for a wardrobe!

Nancy and George left *River Heights Magazine* with more questions than answers. Some lunch, they agreed, might help to sort out the many confusing events of the morning. Hannah Gruen, the Drews' housekeeper, was away so they'd have the house to themselves.

The girls were delighted Carson Drew was home, and Nancy greeted him with a peck on the cheek. Carson sat at the head of the dining room table, surrounded by stacks of manila file folders.

"Why are you home, Dad?" Nancy asked.

"They're preparing for the Christmas party at the office, and it's too hectic," Carson responded.

Nancy went upstairs to change her clothes while George described the incident at the loading dock.

"I have to say I'm rather concerned about your safety in this investigation," Carson said to Nancy when she returned.

"I promise I'll be careful, Dad," she said earnestly. "By the way," she added, "have you ever heard of a Swiss company called Geissbuhler?"

"Hmmm," Carson thought for a moment. "I don't think so. But it's easy enough for me to do a profile on them and get back to you on what business they're in."

"That'd be terrific," Nancy said gratefully.

"How about Perfect Printing here in River Heights, Mr. Drew?" George asked. "Can you tell us anything about their reputation?"

"The Teal family has run that shop since I was a boy. They're contracted to print newspapers, mostly, and are very successful. Mr. Teal turned the business over to his son a few years ago when Stuart graduated from college. I've heard he's one of our best and brightest young businesspeople. Very energetic and aggressive about getting new accounts for the company. What did *you* think of him?"

"He's been cooperative and we've found out the basics about printing from him, but now we need the specifics on how *money* is printed. One lead he gave us, though, could help," Nancy told him.

"There's a printer in Knightsville that prints currency. I'm going to call Chief McGinnis to see if he'll contact the Knightsville people and ask them to meet with us. Plus I'll let him know about the 'accident' on the loading dock," she assured her father.

The drive out to National Printing Arts took longer than expected because of heavy traffic. A winter storm watch was sending most people home early from work.

When they finally arrived at three o'clock, Nancy and George were greeted by Charles Nemo, the head of public affairs.

Whereas the mood at Perfect Printing had been friendly and casual earlier that day, National Printing Arts was formal. Nancy and George were required to wear visitors' passes. Mr. Nemo apologized for the rule but explained that procedures at the plant had to be strict because they printed currency.

"Can we start with the basics?" Nancy asked. "How do you make *real* money?"

"Become a doctor or a lawyer—I'd say they make real money!" Nemo joked. Nancy was glad their guide had a sense of humor.

"Seriously, Miss Drew," he said, "you'll understand that a significant portion of what we do here is secret. But I'll be glad to give you a basic outline. Exhibit A," he declared as he drew a one-dollar bill from his wallet. "Real paper money is made from metal plates that are engraved with the image of the bill. Many engravers have a hand in making the plate; as many as thirty-seven different craftspeople can be involved. That way, no one person knows the secret of the whole engraving process.

"Your average counterfeiter uses a much simpler process. He—or she—takes a photo of a bill on fine-grain film. Then they doctor the negative to get a good-looking Treasury seal—the green circle that says the Department of the Treasury."

Nancy and George peered at the money. "The seal is one of the trickiest parts," Nemo went on. "But let's say you get that right and have realistic-looking artwork ready to print; you still need three more important pieces. You need a way to reproduce the bills—a printing press. You need good ink. And finally, you need realistic-looking paper."

George looked down at the bill and traced the image of George Washington. "Making money is a lot more complicated than spending it," she quipped. Now it was Nancy and Nemo's turn to laugh.

"When it's done properly, the process is quite straightforward," Nemo said. "Real currency is printed on one kind of printing press: an offset press. The right ink comes from a single company. And the right paper is made by only one firm here in the States: King & Company."

"If the combination of right ingredients is so tricky, then how do counterfeiters come up with realistic-looking bills?" Nancy wondered aloud.

"Good question," Nemo answered. "And you'll be amazed at the number of different techniques people use. It would take me weeks to list all the tricks for you. But there are a couple of popular ones, such as amateur use of color copy machines, which are extremely common now."

"I didn't realize they were common," Nancy admitted. Therefore Chloe's machine wasn't unusual. But why did she have it stashed in the closet?

"This is another one," Nemo said. "Some pros use offset printing presses. Then, to get around the paper problem, they bleach one-dollar bills to remove the ink. And it works! Then, once they've got bleached-out bills, they reprint the money in higher denominations, say, twenties, fifties, and hundreds, on the same paper!"

Nancy finished writing and looked up from her notebook. "You've been incredibly helpful," she said gratefully.

"Feel free to call and ask questions if you need to," Nemo replied. Nemo moved to the door, signaling the session was over.

Once outside, Nancy and George were eager to stretch their legs before starting the trip home.

"Real-looking art to print the bills. A printing press to reproduce them. Good ink. Good paper," Nancy repeated.

"Yup, those seem to be the big four," George agreed. "Well, Stuart has printing presses galore, so maybe we'd better do more with the paper and ink side of it as well as finding out who's making the original artwork."

"That's it! I'm glad you reminded me!" Nancy said enthusiastically. "When we were with Stuart this morning, I nabbed some paper just in case we needed it."

"Now's the time to check it out," George said eagerly.

Nancy produced the letterhead and held it up to the weak winter sun. With the late rays illuminating the watermark—the paper manufacturer's nearly invisible name—she and George could just make out the company name on the fine-grade stock. Simultaneously, both girls let out a gasp. Written in capital letters, subtly but unmistakably, was the name of the company that produced the paper: KING & COMPANY.

Chapter

Six

"THERE'S ONE THING we know for sure," George said as she leaned back on the Drews' sofa. "All our suspects either have color copiers or have access to one. And they all own expensive stuff. Pamela's clothes. Jason's car, even if he did buy it secondhand. And Stuart's clothes prove he's got money. So everyone's guilty on that account. But Stuart's the only one with King paper."

The girls were at Nancy's house, brainstorming.

"Why don't you come right out and ask Stuart what he's using the paper for, Nan. There's probably some logical reason, and it'll save us a lot of work if we know what it is. Besides, it seems like he'd tell you just about anything!"

George jibed, bringing up Stuart's obvious crush on Nancy.

"Here's what we've got to zero in on," Nancy said, avoiding the issue of romance. "Does it *really* mean anything that Stuart has access to King paper? Can he get his hands on King *currency* paper as well?"

"Good question. There must be a way to find out—"

Nancy snapped her fingers. "I've got it!" she said, and picked up the phone. She eyed George as she punched the buttons.

"Good afternoon. This is Nancy Drew calling for Stuart Teal," she said confidently. "Hi, Stuart," she said moments later. "No, my wrist doesn't hurt too much. I bet it'll be completely better by tomorrow. Um-hmmm. My left wrist." She rolled her eyes at George as if to dismiss Stuart's attentions. "Actually I wondered if you could do me a favor. I finally came up with an idea for a Christmas present for my friend Bess. I thought she'd love stationery with her name and address on the top. The problem is, I don't know if any printer could get the job done by Saturday." She paused and looked at George, who gave her a thumbs-up sign. "You would? Well, thank you very much. Okay, I'll give you the address." She dictated the information. "And the design can be simple, just black script on white paper.

By the way, what kind of paper will you be using?" She plopped down into a chair. "Oh," she said, faking innocence, "I didn't know King's was the finest available. That'll be great then. They make the paper money's printed on? What a coincidence! If it's good enough for Uncle Sam, it's good enough for me!"

Nancy picked up a pencil and wrote the words *dead end* on a piece of paper. She flashed the message to George. It didn't necessarily mean anything that Stuart used King paper since it was known as quality stationery; it would only be unusual if Stuart had King & Company *currency* paper.

Suddenly Nancy snapped to attention. "Racquetball? Tonight? Hold on. I'll check with George."

Nancy put her hand over the mouthpiece and whispered, "Do you want to go? It'll be you, me, Stuart, and Jason."

"Definitely," George whispered back. "It'll give us a chance to snoop some more." Nancy made the date for seven o'clock and hung up.

She ran upstairs and grabbed her sports bag. In the two hours before meeting Stuart and Jason, she and George would attempt to question both Celeste and Pamela.

Nancy packed her blue nylon gym bag with shorts, a T-shirt, athletic shoes, and racket. She stepped into the bathroom for the toiletries she'd need for her shower afterward. Nancy caught herself debating about what makeup to bring. She didn't want Stuart to see her a mess. Why am I so worried about what Stuart thinks? she asked herself. Especially when I have Ned. But she knew the answer: She was beginning to like Stuart.

Nancy felt relieved that Stuart had a good excuse for stocking King paper. Stuart was looking more and more honest as the investigation progressed, and Nancy allowed herself to feel excited about the evening ahead.

The mood at *River Heights Magazine* was frantic. "You've got to excuse the craziness around here. We're trying to finish an issue before the holiday," Celeste explained.

"I was just hoping to get a bit of information on Pamela Carrera, the one who gave you cash for that ski trip," Nancy explained. "How long have you known her?"

Celeste was thoughtful. "I'd say six months or maybe seven. She came to *River Heights Magazine* from one of the fashion magazines."

"How's she been getting along with the staff here?" Nancy continued. "Any problems?"

"Well, now that you mention it," Celeste offered, "it has taken her some time to adjust. She was running up the expense account for her department. Too many client lunches and what not. But I'm sure it's just because she was used to bigger budgets," Celeste added kindly.

Before Nancy could question Celeste further, she was interrupted by a loud knock. "Come in," Celeste called.

The door flew open and a young woman popped her head in. "Celeste, Susan needs you to look at the mock-ups *now.*"

Celeste sprang up from her desk chair and flew out the door, calling back to Nancy and George, "Terribly sorry, I can't talk any more. Can you see yourselves out? Great."

Nancy trailed Celeste with her eyes, making sure she was well out of the vicinity before moving.

"One thing before we go," Nancy said, shooting around the desk to Celeste's chair.

"I'll be on the lookout," George offered, closing the heavy door to a mere crack.

A piece of paper bearing Chloe Lee's logo had caught Nancy's attention. She pushed aside a pile of papers on Celeste's desk, exposing a nine-by-twelve envelope with Chloe's full return address. When Nancy held it up for inspection, the unsealed envelope fell open and a blank letter with a check attached with a paper clip slipped out. The check stated in block letters the amount and the recipient: Chloe was giving ten thousand dollars to Celeste!

Nancy did a rapid double take, making sure she counted the number of zeroes correctly. She replaced the check in the envelope and half-buried it under the sheaf of papers.

Returning to the other side of the desk, Nancy signaled George to leave, wondering why in the world Chloe had paid Celeste that much money.

The art director motioned the girls to go inside her office. "Have a seat," she offered. "And I should tell you I'm sorry I wasn't here for our appointment earlier. I had a work emergency," Pamela said, smiling nervously.

"No problem," Nancy said smoothly. "We just wondered if you'd thought any more about the ski trip money and where it might have come from. Any ideas?" There was an awkward silence.

"The ski trip money," Pamela repeated. "I gave it my best shot, and I can't think where it could have come from. I mean, think of all the places you go in a day. I'll show you." Pamela flipped open her datebook and began turning pages. "The ski trip was the twelfth of November and the money had to be in two weeks before. So that puts us at the end of October." She peered over her datebook and held Nancy's gaze. Nancy felt that Pamela had been doctoring her story.

"Now, in the last two days of October, these are the places I went and spent money," she said, reading from her book. "The manicurist, the post office, the costume rental shop for a Halloween costume, the florist, the video store." She paused. "And those are just the places I wrote down in my book," she emphasized.

"I see," said Nancy. There was no point in arguing with Pamela. The only alternative would be a direct confrontation.

"Let's talk about your position here, for a moment. What can you tell us about your spending habits during the past six months? Have you been overreaching your budget a bit?" Nancy asked.

"What are you saying?" Pamela shot back, "and who have you been talking to?"

"We're trying to find out who in River Heights is making counterfeit money," George answered. "By helping us with information, you might clear your name."

Pamela seemed frightened. "Look, maybe I have been spending a little too much too quickly. But I've pulled back lately, okay? And furthermore, my spending habits are none of your business." Pamela was red with rage now.

Nancy realized there were no more questions left for Pamela to answer. If she wanted better answers, she'd have to dig deeper.

An hour later Nancy and George were at the River Heights Athletic Club, jockeying for position. George and Jason made a fearsome racquetball team, both playing aggressively. Nancy enjoyed being Stuart's partner. He was careful to give Nancy the opportunity to participate fully in the game. In his short-sleeved T-shirt and running shorts, Stuart looked more muscular than he had in a suit.

When the last point was won, Jason threw up his arms and made the victory sign. "Fabulous game, partner," he said to George. "And I played brilliantly, if I do say so myself. I only wish Chloe could see me now," he puffed, wiping the sweat from his face with a towel.

"What's Chloe up to tonight?" George asked casually.

"Deadline," Stuart and Jason replied at the same time, and laughed. How strange that both of them said *deadline,* Nancy thought.

As they headed for the locker rooms, Stuart told Nancy in a confidential tone, "You were a terrific partner. I'm sorry we didn't win!"

Nancy blushed at the compliment. "It was my fault," she said. "I need some practice."

"Stu, let's hit the showers," Jason called from up ahead. "These gals may want to take a turn in the steam room. It's women's night," he added, noting the sign on the steam room door as they passed. "You can take a few minutes in there," he said. "There'll be enough time."

"All right," Nancy said.

"The club's closing in half an hour, so if you aren't back here by then, we'll send the police in after you!" Stu said.

"Don't worry, we'll be ready," Nancy assured him. She and George slipped into the locker room and emerged minutes later, clad only in towels.

"This is *exactly* what we needed," Nancy said, setting the dial of the circular timer for five minutes.

"How great to have the whole thing to ourselves," George said as bursts of steam poured in from spigots overhead. The girls had to grope their way through the mist to find a place to sit.

Nancy settled herself on the plastic bench lining the rear wall. George was already stretched out on the adjacent seat.

Far too soon, it seemed, the timer buzzed. The girls rose and reluctantly walked to the door. Nancy reached to push it open and found the handle didn't turn.

"That's strange," she said. "These things never

lock." She jiggled the handle twice more, then turned to George.

"You give it a try," she suggested. George took over. As steam continued to fill the room, the temperature escalated and Nancy felt as though she were on fire.

George had no better luck. They were obviously locked in. "Nan," George said, with a catch in her voice, "we're going to pass out if we stay in here much longer."

"You're right," Nancy agreed. "We've got to figure something out *now.*" Their need to escape was urgent: The steam room was getting hotter by the second!

Chapter

Seven

"Let's try pounding on the door. Maybe someone will hear us," George suggested.

"Okay. On the count of three, start pounding," said Nancy. Both girls made fists and beat on the door for almost a minute. The exertion was costly; they were losing strength.

"It's no use," Nancy said, "I'll have to kick it down." To get a running start, she walked four paces to the back wall of the chamber. Then she clutched the towel around her with one hand and extended her other arm out to the side for balance. She moved swiftly forward and raised her right leg to kick it open. Just then the door swung out.

Nancy fell forward, clutching the towel to her

chest. She staggered into the corridor. The rush of cooler air made her dizzy, so she put her head between her knees to avoid fainting. George, close behind, followed suit.

"What happened in there?" a startled voice cried out. It was Stuart, who was holding a crowbar. Jason and Marco were beside him.

"Couldn't get out—door stuck," Nancy panted.

"We heard this incredible racket coming from in there," Stuart said. "I tried opening the door but it was locked. Then I realized something must be wrong. So I got this." He held up the crowbar.

"Tonight's just full of surprises," said Jason, glancing at Marco. "When did you turn up, pal?"

"I come here every day," Marco said, sounding defensive. "I work out. I just don't play racquetball."

"Take it easy," Jason told Marco. "Never mind. Whatever happened, everybody seems to be okay now," he pronounced.

Stuart stared affectionately at Nancy and gave her arm a squeeze. Once again, she felt a tingling at his nearness. She turned away from him in embarrassment and wished she could control her feelings, at least until the case was solved and Ned returned.

Feeling light-headed, more questions buzzed

through her brain. Could the door really have been jammed? Or was someone trying to lock them in? And worst of all, could Stuart Teal be responsible?

The next morning Nancy woke early and checked the thermometer outside her window before getting dressed. It was six below and overcast, probably too cold to snow. She remembered that that night was the cartoonists' society dinner.

After eating breakfast, Nancy lounged on the sofa in the den, clipboard in hand. She began drawing up a list of her next moves. Would Stuart be capable of counterfeiting, she wondered, thinking about how kind he'd been to her. Perfect Printing was thriving. What would motivate him to need more money? I just don't have enough information, she thought resolutely. In Pamela's case, Nancy felt it was time to home in on her suspect's spending. She'd phone a few of the boutiques Pamela frequented to find out how she paid for her purchases. If she was the counterfeiter, she'd be paying with cash.

Then there was Chloe's studio to check out. Surely Chloe must have a record explaining the ten-thousand-dollar check, she thought. Nancy made a mental note to drive by the studio at the next possible opportunity.

Celeste hadn't been too helpful; she was either genuinely busy or trying to hide something. And so far Marco was nearly a total mystery. He was unhappy and disgruntled, but was it over Chloe's lack of attention or money matters? There had to be some way of getting more information on him.

Nancy decided to try to call Marco and Chloe's old design school. She was sure to find out something interesting. Nancy grabbed the Chicago phone book from the shelf and searched for the school's number. After being transferred several times, she reached the alumnae department.

"I'm sorry," a bureaucratic voice on the other line informed her. "All alumnae inquiries of a nonacademic nature must be made in person." Nancy hung up and thought for a moment. Driving to the school would take valuable time, but Nancy had a hunch it would be worth the effort. She called George to invite her on a trip to the big city.

The trip took less than an hour door to door. Nancy felt exhilarated to be driving into Chicago.

According to the city map, the School of Design was fifteen blocks from the Museum of Science and Industry. Nancy knew the route to the museum by heart; ever since she was a child, she'd been going there.

George guided them directly to the entrance of the School of Design. Life-size bronze sculptures stood staring out at a semicircular expanse of lifeless brown grass that buffered the building from the main road.

After mounting the steep front steps, they made their way down a long hallway. The graphic arts department was unmistakable: It had a large, clear, elegantly lettered sign.

"Excuse me," Nancy said to the receptionist. "We're trying to get in touch with a teacher of ours in this department. He was on staff five years ago," she began.

"Five years ago," the receptionist repeated. "That'll be tough. You must mean Max Leach. He was here until a few years ago but he's retired now. What do you need him for?"

"We just wanted to say hi," Nancy improvised. "He was our teacher. We thought it would be great to surprise him. Would you have his address?" Nancy pressed.

"I've got it," answered the young man, "but I'm not supposed to give it out. Sorry."

"I totally understand. Thanks anyway," Nancy said quickly. She nodded to George and hurried out of the office and down the hallway. Nancy stopped short when she came to a pay phone.

"What's up, Nan? Why are we stopping? We've got to get the guy's address."

"And we will," Nancy replied, lifting the phone receiver and punching some numbers. "We've got the guy's name. And if we're lucky, he still lives in the city." She asked the operator for the telephone number for Max Leach. She was in luck and got it. Then she called her dad in River Heights and asked him to use his *Cole's Reverse Directory* to locate the address for Max Leach's phone number.

Max Leach's address was within walking distance of the school. He'd probably had the apartment during all the years of his teaching, Nancy guessed.

Nancy and George quickly covered the six blocks to Max Leach's apartment building. Stepping into the building's vestibule, they searched the directory panel for the name Leach and found it next to the letters PH for penthouse.

To their surprise, they were buzzed in without being questioned over the intercom. They rode the elevator up, got out, and then rang the doorbell.

After a moment, a middle-aged woman with bobbed hair and clear plastic glasses appeared at the door. She appeared shocked to see the girls. "Oh, my," she said, "I assumed you were the cable TV repairman we called." Just as she spoke, a pair of wire-haired terriers raced to the door and began barking wildly at the intruders.

70

"Edith! Ozzie!" she commanded the canines. "Settle down now." The animals obediently stopped barking but continued to wag their tails frantically.

"Now then," she said, addressing Nancy, "what can I do for you?"

"I'm Nancy Drew, and this is George Fayne. We'd like to ask Professor Leach a few questions. It's about some former students of his," she explained.

"Well, I don't know. Oh, all right, you look harmless enough. Come right in," she said pleasantly. "Max," she called. "Ma-a-a-ax!"

"I'm here, Rebecca dear." A tall, slim man strode into the living room. With perfect posture and straight jet black hair, he hardly looked old enough to have stopped working.

When they finished the introductions, Nancy briefed the former teacher on her background as a detective. Without mentioning the details, she told Mr. Leach that she was working on a case involving his former students.

"Do you remember Marco Diani and Chloe Lee?" she asked.

"Of course I remember them." He chuckled. "It would be impossible not to. Those were two of the most talented kids ever to enter my program—my former program," he corrected himself.

"What was special about them?" Nancy probed.

"They were *original*," Leach said quickly, "and professional. You know, that young woman did the first sketches of Penny the Dog in one of my classes," he said proudly. "Chloe knew what she wanted to do and how to do it even then. She was an ambitious person and very determined," he added. Determined to play by the rules or determined to get rich by creating counterfeit money if she needed it? Nancy wondered.

"And what about Marco?" George put in, hoping to get the elder man's insight.

"Good question," he said. "What *about* Marco? He was pretty much a mystery to me—a very introverted young man. But those two were completely inseparable. He hung on to Chloe the way a shipwrecked man hangs on to his dinghy. At first they were boyfriend and girlfriend, I believe," he added. "I remember thinking what a nice-looking young couple they made."

Nancy and George exchanged glances. That could explain why Marco was so jealous of Jason.

"But that didn't last long," Leach continued, "though they did remain close friends. The boy's language skills weren't very good, and Chloe seemed to take care of him. She was older, had more confidence. It was a shock to me what eventually happened. A sad story, really." He paused to remove a handkerchief from his pocket and blow his nose.

"What exactly happened?" Nancy asked, eager for a break in the case. The professor took his time answering. "You've got to understand, he's the best craftsperson I've ever encountered. He had a natural ability to draw. *And* paint. *And* do graphic design. He could have done anything he wanted in the commercial art world," he said, shaking his head sadly.

"But instead what did he do?" Nancy prompted.

The professor met Nancy's gaze directly. "He got into hot water. Over his head. Got himself expelled in his sophomore year!"

"How did that happen?" asked Nancy, surprised that the timid Marco could have gotten into so much trouble.

"Because he wasted all his talent," Leach said bitterly. "He decided to make counterfeit money on a desktop printer!"

Chapter

Eight

"THAT'S AWFUL!" George exclaimed. "Did he get in trouble with the police?"

"Big time," Leach explained, "but he was young—only seventeen, though advanced for his age. And it was his first offense. If I remember correctly, he spent several months in a juvenile detention center."

"Why do you think he did it in the first place?" asked Nancy.

Leach replied, "I've asked myself that at least a thousand times. I think he did it for the challenge. I think he was testing his skill. He wanted to see if the bills he made could pass. I also believe he was naive enough to think he wouldn't get in trouble. All he did was comp up a few twenties. He used them in the school cafeteria. If he'd had a larger scheme in mind, he'd have printed up enough cash to buy himself a car or something. . . ."

Nancy stood, signaling that she had the information she needed.

"If you see the young man," Leach said, "wish him good luck for me."

"Sure will," Nancy told him, shaking his hand heartily. And he's going to need all the luck in the world, she thought grimly.

"These cartoonists sure know how to throw a party!" George said happily as she and Nancy entered the grand ballroom of the Barrington Hotel.

"Welcome to the Fourteenth Annual Cartoonists Dinner." The voice came from a person dressed in a fuzzy dog suit. Nancy turned and recognized the character as Penny the Dog. He extended a paw for her to shake. Nancy and George laughed.

An enormous mirrored ball hung in the center of the room, sending tiny glints of light dancing around the walls and ceiling. To Nancy, every physical detail of the party was dazzlingly witty. Each centerpiece featured a colorful cutout of a different cartoon character.

Glancing around the ballroom, Nancy could see that she and George were appropriately dressed for the gala. "I'm glad we asked what to wear," Nancy commented. She felt ultrafeminine in her black velvet pouf dress. Its sweetheart neckline created a dramatic contrast against her fair skin; the gently rounded skirt highlighted her shapely legs. She wore the sheerest black stockings, reserved for formal occasions, and black patent leather shoes with a slim, graceful heel.

George looked smart in silvery evening pants and coordinating scoop-necked top and gold-braid piping. She seemed even taller than usual, having chosen a moderate heel to go with the ensemble. A soft silver eye shadow and subtle pink lip gloss accented her lively features.

As the two girls walked toward the table with the seating cards, Nancy sensed eyes on her and George and saw nods of approval from the people around her.

Next, the girls made their way to their seats, which were just to the side of the stage. No sooner had they arrived at their table than a waiter in tails approached them with a tray of hors d'oeuvres. "Can I interest you ladies in a hot dog? Hamburger?" he asked, smiling and lowering the tray. Nancy and George saw perfectly formed franks and hamburgers in buns—only they were miniature! What a wonderful idea, Nancy thought.

After they helped themselves, the waiter politely pulled out their chairs to seat them. An elegantly wrapped party favor sat at each girl's place.

"Should we?" Nancy asked George, holding up the small package and wondering out loud if they should open them.

"Why not?" suggested George and began unwrapping her gift. Inside was a copy of Chloe's latest series of cartoons, a small comic book called *Penny the Dog at the North Pole*. Nancy nodded her approval.

Just then she noticed Stuart, who had come up beside her. He smiled broadly at Nancy and kissed her on the cheek. Then he gathered her hands in his and stepped back as if to get a more complete view of her. "You look exceptionally lovely, as I knew you would."

"Thank you, Stuart," Nancy murmured. And you look exceptional, too, she thought, not trusting herself to say so when she was feeling so giddy. In his tuxedo, Stuart was handsomer than ever.

From the corner of her eye, Nancy could see Chloe waving at them excitedly. Jason, she noticed, was lagging behind, he and Marco deep in conversation.

After greeting Chloe and congratulating her for

her nomination, Stuart said, "It's a good thing we're near the podium—it'll make it easier for you to collect your award!"

"Don't be too sure I'm going to win," Chloe lamented. "There's talent here that's been around a lot longer than I have."

Stuart started to protest, but the emcee began to speak. It was the person dressed in the dog costume. Instead of asking the assembled guests to quiet down, the live cartoon dog began barking into the microphone.

"These cartoon people are hilarious!" George whispered. Nancy nodded.

"We all know why we're here tonight," the emcee continued. "We're here for the free meal!" he joked, and the audience chuckled. "Seriously," he went on, "tonight we're here to honor the best of our profession. To bestow the annual award on the one cartoonist in Illinois whose work has been the most fun and made the greatest number of people laugh the hardest. We'll get to all that after we enjoy the wonderful meal that's about to be served. So you nominees will just have to wait. Ha-ha!"

After four elaborate courses and dessert, the host took his place once again on the brightly lit stage. "Now, it's my pleasure to announce to you the names of our nominees for Cartoonist of the Year. They are Barbara Genovese, Howard Belk,

Neil Osterberg, and last, but certainly not least, Chloe Lee."

While the applause after each nominee was enthusiastic, the crowd went wild after Chloe's name was read. Chloe was sitting with her eyes closed, her fingers crossed for good luck. Jason had his arm wrapped around her, his fingers crossed as well. Nancy smiled at the sweet image.

Nancy caught Marco's gaze, and for the first time, he looked her straight in the eye and nodded. Slightly surprised, Nancy smiled and nodded back. Maybe Marco was warming to her, she thought.

"And the winner is," he glanced down at the card, "Chloe Lee!"

The cartoonist popped out of her seat and let out a delighted hoot. She hugged Jason before she walked onto the stage to accept her prize and give her acceptance speech.

When she returned, Marco turned to Chloe and gave her a peck on the cheek. "It's wonderful for you," he said. He sounded sincere, Nancy thought.

"It *is* wonderful for us, isn't it?" Jason said deliberately, "and maybe when you're all grown up, Marco, you'll get an award, too."

The table fell silent. Marco glared at Jason, then he slowly rose and threw his napkin down on the table.

"I have had enough of this—this nonsense," Marco sputtered. "I have acknowledged you and Chloe being together. What must I do to convince you I am not jealous? You have no right to bother me about this any more. It is completely unacceptable to me." Before Chloe could speak up to mediate, he stormed off.

Ten minutes later, Nancy excused herself to go to the ladies' room. George followed, commenting, "Those guys really go at it!"

"I'll say," Nancy said, "and it's time we got to the bottom of it. What do you say we take a trip to the studio later on to look around? Chloe's in seventh heaven; there's no way she'll go back there to work tonight. And Marco seemed too mad to want to work later."

"It's worth a try," George agreed.

In the hallway outside, Stuart intercepted them. "I'll see you back at the table," George said hurriedly, leaving Nancy and Stuart alone.

"Great," Nancy called after her. "Those two argue so much. Why is that?" Nancy asked Stuart, referring to Marco and Jason.

"I hate to say it," Stuart said slowly, "but I think it has to do with love." He touched Nancy's face lightly as he talked. "Marco was deeply in love with Chloe, and she's with Jason now. He never got over her, and now he wants them to be as miserable as he is. I wouldn't be surprised if you found love—not money—at the bottom of this crime."

"Are you saying you think Marco is the counterfeiter? And that he's trying to frame Chloe to get revenge?" Nancy asked. Stuart stopped stroking Nancy's face and gently placed his hands on her shoulders. "I'm not positive," Stuart told her earnestly. "But I can tell you one thing for sure—"

Nancy felt her heart flutter. "What's that?" she asked, trying to keep her tone businesslike.

Gliding his hands down Nancy's arms, he replied, "People will do almost anything for love. After meeting you, I can speak as an expert on that subject!"

Later that night at Chloe's studio, George shone a flashlight on the lock on the outside door.

Nancy picked the lock with a long, thin metal tool she had mined from her purse. In less than thirty seconds, the lock opened with a click.

It was easy to spot Marco's work station: His was the only tidy area in the office.

"He sure is neat," George observed.

"Yeah, and he sure has expensive stuff," Nancy noticed, gingerly picking up a cordless phone. "And a personal CD player. I saw one like this when we were shopping for Ned's Christmas present. We're talking big bucks for this model."

"This stuff may be expensive, but that doesn't do us much good. Maybe there are more clues on the computer," George suggested.

"It's worth a try," Nancy agreed.

George sat down and switched on the computer's toggle switch. Luckily, the software didn't require a password. A menu with at least fifty options appeared on the screen.

Nancy traced the selections with her finger. "Let's just take a look," she murmured, then read out some file names in alphabetical order. "Samsondale—that wouldn't be it . . . Shonteff Corporation—probably not . . . *soldi!*" she said excitedly.

George studied the screen. "What is it, Nan?"

"Just a sec," her friend responded. "Let's see if I can get this to work." She took over for George and studied the directions flashing on the bottom of the screen. "Press F-six to scroll down," she said to herself.

"Come on, Nan, what does *soldi* mean?" George persisted.

"It means money—in Italian!" Nan told her. As she uttered the words, an image came up on the screen: It was a true-to-size computerized image of a fifty-dollar bill!

Chapter

Nine

Gosh!" George cried out. "I think we've got our counterfeiter!"

"This looks bad, George, but it's not solid evidence," Nancy lamented.

"I see what you mean," George responded. "Somehow we've got to catch Marco in the act."

"If he's guilty, that is," Nancy pointed out as she shut off the computer.

"I just know there's something here we've missed, but I can't put my finger on it," Nancy said as they walked back to the car.

"Let's sleep on it and come back tomorrow," George offered as she stifled a yawn.

* * *

Nancy awoke early the next morning, determined to return to the studio.

She showered, then dressed in black leggings and an oversize turtleneck sweater.

Carson Drew was sitting in the breakfast nook reading the newspaper when Nancy came downstairs. Hearing his daughter's footsteps, Carson said good morning. "You certainly got in late last night. How was the dinner?"

Nancy gave him the details of the previous evening, describing everything from the centerpieces to the food and the award. She tried not to mention Stuart too much in her stories.

"I have something to report back," Carson said, folding the paper thoughtfully and tucking it under his plate. "This could be interesting for you. I've checked on that Swiss firm you mentioned to me, the Geissbuhler Company. They manufacture ink—the kind of ink that's used to print money. You'll find Geissbuhler products at a security printing plant."

"Hmm," Nancy said. "That *is* interesting. And I'm dying to know what Stuart Teal has to say about it!" She jumped up from her chair.

"Where are you off to without breakfast?" Nancy's father asked.

"To find a couple of guys who have an awful lot to answer to!" Nancy replied. The time had come to confront Mr. Diani and Mr. Teal.

Nancy's mind whirred. Stuart's involvement with the Geissbuhler Company certainly seemed suspicious. But the evidence against Marco was even stronger. To make matters worse, she still had no reason for Chloe's check to Celeste or Pamela's huge payments to River Heights's finest clothing stores.

Nancy pulled into George's driveway and honked the horn. George bounded out the front door and into the Mustang.

"It's freezing! I think the Ice Age is coming!" George said, pulling off her gloves and holding her hands up to the heating vent.

"It'll probably snow in the next couple days," Nancy commented. "I hope in time for a white Christmas."

She told George about Stuart and the Geissbuhler Company. Then she continued, "The light on my answering machine was flashing three times, so I thought there were three calls. But when I listened to the tape, each one was a hangup. Someone's trying to get through to me. It could be a warning."

When they pulled up to the studio, Nancy and George noticed only one car in the parking lot. Nancy parked next to it and killed the ignition.

"That's strange. The lot looks awfully empty."

George glanced at her watch. "It *is* only eight forty-five, Nan."

Nancy rang the studio bell, and Chloe answered it in an instant.

"It's you!" she exclaimed, disappointed. "I—I mean I was waiting for Marco. I don't know where he is—"

"May we come in?" Nancy asked politely, stamping her feet to ward off the cold. "Sorry to come by so early. You must be exhausted after all the excitement last night."

"I haven't had time to be," Chloe confided, opening the door wide to admit Nancy and George.

Chloe settled them in the conference room and explained the situation. "Marco had an eight o'clock deadline for a client this morning—a dog food manufacturer. He was supposed to have had mechanicals for them at the meeting. But he never showed up." Her voice was filled with emotion.

"Does he often miss deadlines? And is he usually late?" Nancy probed.

"Never," Chloe said quickly. "How do you think he got this far? He *never* misses a deadline. I don't know where he could be." The cartoonist's eyes filled with tears. "It's just not like him."

"Did you call him at home?" Nancy asked.

"I tried," Chloe said. "And I talked with

Giovanni, Marco's roommate. He checked Marco's bedroom. There was no sign of him."

"Did Giovanni say whether Marco had been home last night?" Nancy asked.

"He couldn't tell," Chloe said. "Giovanni said he got in really late and went straight to bed. When he looked in Marco's room, he couldn't tell if the bed had been slept in."

The office phone rang shrilly. "That may be him," Chloe said. "I'll be right back."

While Chloe was gone, George whispered, "Either she's a really great actress or she doesn't know where Marco is. I think she's telling the truth. I feel sorry for her!"

"Me, too," Nancy replied, "but I'd feel a lot sorrier if I knew what that ten-thousand-dollar check was for and what Marco was doing with the graphic of a fifty-dollar bill on his computer!"

Chloe returned, more concerned than ever. "That was Jason," she said. "He has no idea where Marco is. I wish I could find him."

"Maybe you can," Nancy began, "if you answer one question."

Chloe perked up. "How?" she asked.

"Tell us why you wrote a check to Celeste for ten thousand dollars," Nancy asked.

Chloe gasped. "How do you know about that?"

"It's my job," Nancy answered.

"Well, I might as well tell you," Chloe said

slowly. "Celeste and I are planning to go into business together. We were thinking about forming a small advertising agency with Marco. He'd do the graphic design, I'd be the illustrator, Celeste was going to be our salesperson, and Jason was going to be the copywriter."

"Was?" Nancy asked. "Isn't that still your plan?"

"That's the problem. Marco was thinking of backing out. At first we were all in it together: Each of us had to put up ten thousand dollars toward start-up costs. I had the money from the Penny the Dog syndication, Celeste makes an okay living as an ad director, Jason is fine for money, and Marco's pretty successful as a freelancer." She frowned when her friend's name came up again.

"Why was Marco trying to back out?" Nancy asked carefully.

"It's ridiculous, really." Chloe sighed. "He doesn't like Jason, and he's upset that Jason and I are going out."

Nancy thought Chloe was telling the truth.

"If this has been building for all these years, why do you think Marco is so angry about it *now?*" asked Nancy.

"I'm not sure, but he has gotten more upset about me and Jason lately," she admitted. Chloe put her hand to her face and began to cry quietly.

Nancy guessed that Marco had been anxious lately because of the counterfeiting investigation. This seemed to be the right time to broach the subject with Chloe. "We had a talk with a professor of yours and Marco's," Nancy ventured. Chloe raised her head. She looked stricken. "We know all about his college counterfeiting episode."

"I can tell you what that was all about," she said quickly.

"That would be helpful," said Nancy.

"Marco did make counterfeit money," she blurted, "but it was just a joke—a dare really. You can't imagine how mortified he was when they arrested him. He didn't mean anything by it."

"Why didn't you or Marco tell me this before?" Nancy said softly.

"Because I was afraid you'd think he was guilty," Chloe admitted.

"What about the image of the fifty-dollar bill on his computer?" George asked.

"What fifty-dollar bill?" Chloe was indignant now.

"We checked out the studio when we found out about Marco's past," George explained. "And that's when we found a replica of a fifty-dollar bill on Marco's computer."

"I'm sure it's not what you think," Chloe

89

insisted. "Marco does ads for the River Heights Bank. It was probably for a campaign he's doing."

"Do you know that for a fact?" Nancy queried.

"No," Chloe confessed. "But Marco's supersmart. He wouldn't make the same mistake twice."

"I hope you're right," Nancy said. "Thanks for being so honest with us. It can only help us find Marco. Give us a call if he shows up here," she added.

"I promise," Chloe said, seeing them to the door.

"I've got a bad feeling about this," Nancy said to George when they were back in Nancy's car. "If Marco's innocent, why did he disappear?"

Nancy glanced through the windshield and noticed a small red, shimmery object dangling from a branch over the windshield. She pointed to it. "What in the world is *that?*"

"We'll know in a minute," George said, and hopped out to retrieve the object.

It was clearly a Christmas tree decoration, a styrofoam ball covered with red sequins. A ribbon encircled the little ball, and from it hung a folded piece of paper.

"Someone went to an awful lot of trouble to make sure we saw this, Nan," George said as she untied the ribbon and removed the small piece of paper. Unfolding it gingerly, she smoothed it out so that both she and Nancy could view it.

"How strange!" Nancy exclaimed, reading the words aloud. " 'Wise up, girl detective. Nothing's perfect at perfect!' "

Chapter

Ten

NANCY EXAMINED THE SHEET of paper closely. "It looks as if a little kid wrote it," she speculated. Suddenly a different idea came to her and she lit up. "Or," she said, "a right-handed person wrote it with her left hand or vice versa!"

Nancy moistened her finger with the tip of her tongue and smeared a corner of one of the letters. "Would you look at that!" she said. "Whoever wrote this used a fountain pen." She held the sheet of paper up to the light. "Oh," she said, "it's plain old photocopier paper."

"You wouldn't expect Marco to use anything that could identify him, did you, Nan?" George asked slyly.

"Marco!" Nancy exclaimed. "You think he's the one who planted the note?"

"Yup." George nodded. "Think about it: He's counterfeited before. And he thought his secret was safe with Chloe. Plus he has her convinced that he was clean."

"And how do we know that he's not?" Nancy said, eager to explore George's line of thinking.

"We don't," George admitted. "But if Marco was innocent, why wouldn't he stick around to defend himself? It makes sense that he wrote the note, Nan, and he stuck it here for us to find so that we'd think Stuart was the bad guy."

"But it doesn't add up," Nancy persisted. "If Marco ran off the fake bills, how did Celeste end up with them?" she demanded.

"That's easy," George improvised. "He passed some on to Chloe so she'd look suspicious and he wouldn't get in trouble."

"I don't know." Nancy hesitated. "When we find him we'll know more. We ought to find out about Stuart's connection to the Geissbuhler Company."

"I don't know, Nan." George giggled. "My hunch is Marco's our man, and you just want to see Stuart again!"

"No way," Nancy protested. But might there

be a tiny bit of truth to George's comment? she asked herself.

Stuart's assistant greeted Nancy and George by name. "Stuart's on the phone with a client right now. But if you wait just a few minutes, he'll be with you shortly," she said. "Please have a seat."

Nancy and George relaxed on the reception room sofa. After five minutes she spotted Stuart in the hallway beyond the reception area's double glass doors. Nancy repositioned herself in order to get a view of who was with him.

The identity of Stuart's "client" was unmistakable: Pamela Carrera! Nancy nudged George. This could be the connection they were looking for: Maybe Pamela was using Perfect Printing as a cover for her counterfeiting!

When Pamela caught sight of Nancy and George, she paled. Looking at Stuart, she wordlessly searched his face for an explanation for finding Nancy and George in Perfect Printing's reception area.

"Oh, forgive me," Stuart said. "Let me introduce you—"

"We've already met, thank you," said Pamela with annoyance. "I didn't know you two were clients of Stuart's." Nancy and George remained quiet.

Stuart filled the silence. *"River Heights Maga-*

zine has been our client for, oh, six years now," he said.

This case has to come together soon, realized Nancy. The graphic arts and printing communities in River Heights were so close-knit that every suspect knew the identity of everybody else, and so the truth about each suspect was destined to emerge.

"Yes," said Pamela. "And Stuart always keeps our business dealings absolutely confidential," Pamela said. The statement seemed to be a warning to Stuart not to discuss her business with Nancy and George. "And I'll leave you all with that thought," Pamela said, walking away.

Once inside his office, Stuart apologized for Pamela. "I have no idea what she was referring to out there. Anyway, how's your investigation going?"

"We're making progress," Nancy said, hedging. "And, actually, we thought you could give us a little more information."

"Shoot, Nancy," Stuart said agreeably.

"Well, what can you tell us about your security system here?" Nancy went on.

"Hold it!" Stuart exploded. "Do you mean to tell me you think *I* am somehow involved in this case?"

"Not you personally," Nancy reassured him.

"But something could be going on here that you don't know about. With an employee, for instance. Or even a client."

"I know my people, including my security people, my employees, *and* my clients. I can tell you in no uncertain terms that none of my employees would ever dabble in or be an accessory to a counterfeiting scheme." He relaxed his intense gaze just a little and lowered his voice. "You have my personal word on that."

Nancy knew he'd said all he was willing to say on the subject—Stuart was stubborn and determined. He was clearly upset that she would consider him or anyone else at Perfect a suspect in the case.

"Okay, Stuart," she said calmly, "I'll back off in a minute. I've got only one more question. What can you tell me about your business relationship with the Geissbuhler Company?"

"Geissbuhler's really complicated. Let me take you out for dinner tonight, and I'll describe the whole thing over a fabulous meal."

"That's not necessary, Stuart," Nancy said, turning to conceal her blushing face.

"You're right. It's not something I have to do. But I'd love to do it anyway. Please say yes?" he asked charmingly.

"All right," Nancy conceded.

"Fantastic." The printer smiled. "I'll pick you up at seven."

"I'll be ready!" Nancy told him. And you'd better be, too—with a darn good explanation, she thought to herself.

Nancy stood in front of her closet debating what to wear. The blue satin jacket is too dressy, she thought, and the gray dress isn't formal enough. Finally she chose a simply cut dark red dress with long sleeves and a V neck, then applied a little rose-colored matte lipstick.

Nancy pulled back her bedroom curtain to see Stuart's car pull into the driveway. She felt a twinge as she thought of Ned but reminded herself that her date with Stuart was simply part of her investigation. She donned her tan camel hair coat, adding black leather gloves and an elegant green silk scarf for color. She took one last look at herself in the mirror and was satisfied: The green tones brought out the red highlights in her strawberry blond hair.

During the drive to the restaurant, Stuart chatted about his work without mentioning the Geissbuhler Company.

When they arrived at the River Heights Bank building, she knew she was in for a special dinner. A four-star restaurant called Philippe's dominated the top floor. It was the most glamorous restaurant in town. The space was circular, and it rotated to give guests a complete view of River Heights and the river.

As they entered the restaurant, heavenly music played in the background. After a minute or so, when the piece ended, the restaurant's diners applauded gently. Scanning the room, Nancy saw the source of the music: a young woman sitting at a harpsichord.

"Isn't that a lovely sound?" Stuart said, smiling.

"It's incredible!" she told him.

After Nancy and Stuart admired the view, the maître d' led them to a reserved table near the window. The waiter appeared just seconds later, and Stuart ordered an extravagant dinner for the two of them. When their appetizers arrived, he seemed ready to address the tension between them.

"So," he said smoothly, "mademoiselle would like to know about the relationship between Perfect Printing and the Geissbuhler Company of Switzerland."

"If it's not too much to ask," Nancy said.

"The Geissbuhler Company sought me out several months ago. They're involved in a heavy marketing effort to drum up business in the United States."

Nancy nodded, savoring her shrimp cocktail.

"They're very sophisticated," Stuart continued. "They have mailing lists of printing firms, organized state by state. They found me on the roster of major Illinois printers." He paused. "I hope that answers your question," he said earnestly. At least part of it, Nancy said to herself, unwilling to share her thoughts with Stuart. It wasn't as though she could come right out and ask him if he was buying currency ink from the Swiss company.

Before Nancy could answer, Stuart shook his head. "It's not easy romancing a detective," he confided, chuckling.

Nancy smiled. She was drawn to Stuart but felt guilty about Ned. Nancy desperately needed to conceal her feelings from Stuart. What could she say, she wondered, to stop the relationship from going further? She thought hard for a moment before responding. "There's something I need to tell you," she began.

Stuart leaned forward and took Nancy's hand, covering it with his own. "Let me guess," Stuart said as he stroked her hand with his thumb. "There's already a man in your life," he stated quietly.

"How did you know?" Nancy could hardly believe that he knew about Ned.

"It was a simple deduction," Stuart answered, smiling. "You're intelligent, energetic, attractive —it only makes sense. But I'm not too worried about it. I want you, Nancy Drew, and I'm willing to do whatever it takes to win you over!"

Chapter

Eleven

A FEW HOURS LATER Nancy slid her key into the lock of her front door. As she entered, she was startled by the ringing of the dining room clock. Its twelve gongs suggested that she should go straight to bed. She hung her coat in the closet, slipped off her shoes, and padded up the stairs. The answering machine light blinked in the dark in her room. Nancy thought of playing the message but chose instead to lie across the bed with her clothes on, staring up at the dark ceiling.

Nancy's memory took over, and she visualized every moment of her evening with Stuart, taking pleasure in recalling the restaurant's elegant decor, the beautiful harpsichord music, the scrumptious food, the intimate conversation. Then there was the kiss. . . .

Nancy felt guilty about Ned as she allowed herself to replay the scene. After dinner Stuart suggested they spend a minute looking at the river. It had been freezing but exhilarating. Stuart had gently pulled Nancy next to him and wrapped his muscular arm around her shoulders to keep her warm. Finally Stuart had turned toward her, gazing at her under the diffuse light of a street lamp. He had moved closer, and Nancy had let herself ease forward into his arms, ready to kiss him, ready to be kissed.

When at last their lips had touched, Nancy felt a wonderful tingling sensation that seemed to last and last. Nancy took a vow right then never to regret that moment; the kiss, even if it was never repeated, was simply too special.

Emerging from her reverie, Nancy sat up slowly and swung her legs over the side of the bed. Snapping back to reality, she pushed the button on the answering machine and began listening to her messages.

"Nancy?" a tremulous voice said. "This is Chloe Lee. Marco's still missing. I still don't have any news at all from him." The illustrator's voice was weepy. "If he doesn't turn up by tomorrow, I'm calling the police. Please call me imme-

diately—day or night—if you find out anything," she implored before the final click.

"Hi, Nan," George's voice rang out. "I've been
thinking hard about the case, and I really think
Marco's our man. Are you free tomorrow morn-
ing to talk? How's nine? I'll come over then.
Anyway, good night, and I hope you had fun with
Stuart Perfect—I mean Stuart Teal," she teased.

Clad in her flannel nightgown, Nancy climbed
into bed and shivered. Drawing the down com-
forter close around her, she rehashed the events
of the day.

Was Stuart telling the truth about the
Geissbuhler Company? She'd check out his story, but her first priority was to find Marco. Did
he flee because he was guilty? Did Chloe know
more about Marco and the counterfeiting than
she was revealing?

Nancy's thoughts wandered back to Stuart and
then to Ned. The two faces competed with each
other as Nancy closed her eyes. The last image,
though, was of Stuart's deep brown eyes; they
were what tugged her gently into a deep, dream-
less sleep.

At five minutes to nine the next morning, the
doorbell rang. Nancy opened the front door to
find George accompanied by a delivery man
holding a large package.

"Nancy Drew?" he inquired.

"Thanks," Nancy said, signing the delivery slip and thanking the messenger.

Nancy ran in and opened the package to reveal two dozen white roses.

"Wait," said George. With a flourish, she removed the card from its envelope and read aloud, " 'I had a wonderful time last night. How about you? Stuart.' Gosh, Nan, this is getting serious!" George exclaimed. "What is going on between you two?"

Nancy turned to prevent George from seeing the color that had suffused her face. "Nothing serious," she said.

"Facts first," George declared. "Did he kiss you?"

Nancy acted as if she was distracted, making a show of searching for her car keys.

"Nan, quit shying away from the subject," George pressed.

"Okay, he kissed me, but it was in the line of duty. He told me what I needed to know about the Geissbuhler Company."

Nancy repeated Stuart's story. Then she told George about Chloe's call from the night before. "We'd better get moving," she urged. "You look up Marco's address while I call Chief McGinnis." She handed George the phone book.

After updating him on the details of the case, she listened for a few moments. "Nothing new on your end?" she finally asked. "No new counterfeit bills have turned up? Definitely, Chief, I'll call you if I need any help. Yes, I'll be careful," she told him before hanging up.

It took nearly half an hour to get to Marco's house. Nancy drove cautiously; the subzero temperatures had frozen whatever moisture was on the road, forming dangerous ice slicks. Once they were within several miles of Marco's home, George pulled out a local map of the area from the Mustang's glove compartment.

"Okay, Nan. We're looking for 304 Farragan Street." George continued to direct Nancy. Soon they pulled into the driveway of number 304, parked the car, and hopped out.

The girls gazed at the house. It was a two-story structure with a wide front porch. There were two doors side by side. Nancy guessed that the house had been converted into a two-family home.

A minute later Nancy was squinting to see the tiny letters on the pair of buzzers between the doors. She pushed the one labeled Diani/Padula —2nd Fl. When no one responded, she tried the next buzzer. Silence. Nancy pulled a lockpick kit from her purse, bent over the front lock, and silently worked until it opened.

A steep stairwell led up. As they proceeded up it, they heard a creaking noise. "This is kind of creepy," George said to Nancy.

Nancy nodded. When they arrived at the top of the steps, she picked the lock to the apartment.

The living room contained little furniture, only a stylish, black upholstered couch, leather directors' chairs, and a glass coffee table with art books stacked on top of it. The room seemed devoid of clues.

Nancy motioned to George to follow her into the kitchen. That, too, was in perfect order. Clean plates and mugs were stacked neatly in the dish drainer. The chrome and glass kitchen table had been wiped clean.

The girls proceeded to the first of the two bedrooms. The colors in it were riotous. The style and condition of the room was nothing like the rest of the apartment. Dirty clothes were piled in small heaps around the room. "This must be Giovanni's room," George observed, "because Marco is Mr. Neat."

"Except for his bed, which Chloe said he never makes," she reminded her friend. In Marco's room a large, unmade bed dominated. George searched the single wooden bureau and found it completely empty. The only other piece of furniture was a small writing desk. "Fountain pens," George murmured, pointing to the desktop.

"Marco may have written that note about Perfect Printing after all," Nancy said.

In the closet Nancy found empty hangers and nothing else. No suitcase. She turned around. "It looks like our friend Marco has skipped town."

Frustrated, Nancy walked out of the bedroom and into the kitchen, where she stopped in front of the square metal trash can. "I hate this part," Nancy said, depressing the pedal of the trash can with her foot and watching the lid pop open. She sat down on the floor and started searching in it for clues. "If we do this in one big blitz it won't be so bad," she told George. "Then we can clean up, get out of here, and find this guy."

"Sounds like a plan," George said. Opening the cupboard beneath the sink, she crouched down and began foraging for a pair of rubber gloves. "This ought to be civilized for at least *one* of us," George said, finding what she was looking for and pulling the yellow gloves over her hands. She joined Nancy at the trash can, sitting cross-legged beside her.

"How did you know these guys had rubber gloves?" Nancy asked as she painstakingly separated the paper garbage from the rest of the refuse.

"You said Marco was Mr. Neat, remember?" George answered.

"Score one more for you," Nancy acknowledged. Maybe George has a better grip on this case, Nancy thought. Could her feelings for Stuart be influencing her judgment, making her miss important information?

Nancy removed a yellow Post-It from the trash and put it in the "save" pile. It had the word *Koshel* or something similar written on it. The paper meant nothing to Nancy, but she planned to show it to Chloe just as soon as she could. Perhaps Marco's business partner could interpret his clues.

As the pile grew, Nancy found her mind wandering. "Wouldn't it be great if we were at a Christmas party right now, drinking hot cider, eating gingerbread cookies—"

"Flirting with Stuart," George offered. Before Nancy could protest, George rose to her feet. "Let's just dump the garbage out so we don't have to reach inside the thing," she suggested. She emptied the contents onto plastic bags they had spread over the floor.

Out poured the remains of the garbage, topped by an unusually large bunch of plastic trash-can liners. "They're so organized they keep spare bags at the bottom of the can," Nancy marveled, picking up the pile of liners. A second later she was paralyzed with amazement. A stack of twenty-dollar bills spilled out from among the plastic bags, and the blurred printing around the Treasury seal showed they were counterfeit!

Chapter

Twelve

AFTER FINDING the fake cash, Nancy and George telephoned Chloe to ask her to meet with them immediately. Chloe agreed, desperate to do anything that would help her find Marco.

Now the three young women were at Nancy's house, sitting on the living room floor surrounding the coffee table and examining the debris salvaged from Marco's trash can.

"Hold on," Chloe said, sounding encouraged for the first time since her friend's disappearance. She held in her hand the yellow Post-It with the cryptic word *Koshel*. "This sounds familiar. Koshel is a place—I'm sure of that."

"Could you find it on a map?" George asked, ready to retrieve the map from Nancy's car.

"It's not a town or anything," Chloe said, thinking out loud. "I've heard this name before. It's something like Koshel Carwash or Koshel Camp. No, it's Koshel Cottages!" Chloe shouted. "It's the place Marco goes sometimes for a rest. I didn't recognize it at first, because he never calls it that. Usually he just says something like 'I'm taking off.'" Chloe shook her head sadly.

"It's okay! We're back on the map!" George said encouragingly. "What else do you know about these trips of his?"

"He always says the place he goes reminds him of Lake Como in Italy, where he went as a little boy. And he likes this place because it has separate little cottages instead of hotel rooms," Chloe told Nancy and George. "Marco needs lots of privacy—he's really an introvert. What else can I tell you?"

"How often does he go on these trips?" Nancy asked.

"Marco's been to Koshel Cottages four or five times this year. I've never gone with him, I guess because Jason would've been too jealous."

"Does he usually just leave his clients and go there, or does he make plans before leaving?" Nancy questioned.

"So far, he's been careful about planning so he wouldn't leave a client in the lurch. This is the first time he's gone AWOL."

"The other times, though, didn't he leave you a phone number when he knew he'd be out of the office?" Nancy pursued.

"Of course," Chloe replied. "We always know where the other person is so we can cover for each other."

"Well, do you still have the number?" Nancy asked.

"I guess I must, somewhere," Chloe answered. She rummaged through her handbag and pulled out her address book. "Here it is: 'Marco's cottage.'" She read the number as Nancy punched in the numbers on a nearby phone.

Nancy talked to the desk clerk at Koshel Cottages and got all the information she needed.

"First of all, the desk clerk says that Marco checked in late last night," Nancy reported.

"Thank goodness," Chloe whispered. "Did you talk to him?"

"I had the clerk ring his room, but there was no answer. I'd better go there and find out why Marco felt he had to run away."

"Where is this place anyway?" George asked, peering over Nancy's shoulder at the notes she'd jotted down.

"It's on Tracey Lake," Nancy said, "about fifty miles north of here. I've been near there with my dad."

Nancy calculated how long the trip would

probably take. If it did snow, it could be two hours to get there, two hours travel time back, and an hour spent at the cottages. If the trip went off without a hitch, she could be back in River Heights by seven-thirty that evening.

Nancy donned her down jacket and boots and took her car keys out of her pocket.

"I know this looks really bad, Marco skipping out like this," Chloe said quietly. "But there's got to be a logical explanation—*besides* his being guilty of anything."

"We're not jumping to any conclusions," Nancy assured her. "And please call George, here at my house, if you hear from Marco in the meantime."

"I'll do whatever you say. Just please, Nancy, find Marco and tell him that whatever's wrong, he can come back and we'll work it out," Chloe said earnestly.

"I'll do my best," Nancy promised before saying goodbye.

George walked Nancy out to her car. Glancing at her friend, Nancy said, "I'd better start driving. It's by far the best lead we've got, and something tells me we'll be able to crack the case when we get Marco to talk."

"I don't know, Nan. Whoever is behind this has tried to hurt you. I don't think it's safe for you to go by yourself," George warned.

"I'll be okay," Nancy told her friend. "Just promise me you'll be here if I need you."

It was snowing lightly when Nancy left the house. The sky was dark gray as if someone had colored it with a lead pencil. Nancy climbed into the car and got it started. She tuned in the radio to an all-news-and-weather station.

The snow became heavier as Nancy traveled northwest toward Tracey Lake. The highway was slick and driving difficult. Another problem, even more frightening, seized her attention. The Mustang kept pulling to the right with a jerking motion. She seemed to be aiming straight ahead, but every few seconds the car lurched.

Easing her foot off the gas, Nancy flicked on her hazard lights and angled the car toward the shoulder of the road. When she finally came to a stop, she glanced out the window. Cars whizzed by, so she scooted over to the passenger side to exit.

An idea popped into her head: If the lurching was going on every few seconds, the problem probably had to do with one of the tires. A few seconds was exactly the time it took for a wheel to make one complete rotation. She crouched beside the front right tire to investigate. Just as she'd guessed, the wheel itself was wobbly—

enough to destabilize the car. Nancy stared more closely. The lug nuts had been loosened, and it may have been done on purpose!

What was the damage meant to do, slow her down or, worse yet, *kill* her? And who could have done it? It must be someone on her suspect list, Nancy reasoned. Even Marco himself could be responsible. But Nancy had driven the Mustang to his apartment and back with no problem at all, so he couldn't have loosened the wheel because he'd already left town. Or could the culprit be someone else, someone who didn't want her to find Marco?

Nancy walked around to the back of the car. She unlocked the trunk and removed a wrench. Fastening it over each nut, she turned them clockwise until she felt the metal tighten. "Whew," she said, stepping back to catch her breath. "That should hold it."

Back in the car she checked the time on the dashboard clock. She'd lost twenty precious minutes repairing the wheel, and the driving itself was much slower than expected. Nancy took a deep breath and steadied her trembling hands before taking off once again for Koshel Cottages.

It was five o'clock before Nancy reached her destination. A full three inches of snow had fallen, coating everything in sight. In the twilight she could see the sign marked KOSHEL peering at her from a large A-frame cottage. That must be the office, she decided, swinging the Mustang into a parking spot. The lot was full; Nancy guessed that many of the visitors were planning to spend the holidays at the hotel.

An enormous moose's head hung over the reception desk. Rough wooden paneling made the office seem darker and smaller than it was. "Hello," Nancy called out. "Anybody here?"

Only silence. Nancy felt strange, as if she were a million miles away from River Heights.

Suddenly she heard a clattering noise, and a youngish man appeared. "Hello there," he said warmly. "I'm sorry, I didn't hear the door. How can I help you?" he inquired. "I'm Harry Segal."

"I'm looking for Marco Diani, a guest who checked in yesterday or today. I just need to know what cottage Mr. Diani is in."

"Hmmm," said the man pensively. "Let's see." He pulled a ledger from the top desk drawer and ran his finger down a column. Nancy nervously glanced at her watch.

Finally the proprietor found the name. "Now I remember. He's a soft-spoken fellow? With black hair?"

"That's him!" Nancy encouraged. She was restless to get going.

"He did indeed get here yesterday. Checked into number fifty-seven."

"How do I get there?" Nancy asked.

"First of all, you take these," Harry said, producing a pair of snowshoes from under the desk, "and follow the path with the blue markers. You'll pass a few cottages on either side of the path, but not many. Your friend's cottage is farther out than most of the bungalows, at the edge of the woods near the lake."

Nancy thanked the owner, carried the snowshoes to a chair, and sat down. Getting into them was no problem, and standing up was also a breeze. But when Nancy began walking, she found herself listing awkwardly from side to side. Using her new footwear felt like walking with tennis rackets attached to her feet!

Observing Nancy's difficulty with the snowshoes, Mr. Segal walked over to the front door and held it open. She trudged over the threshold, thanking him again.

The snow had begun to mix with sleet, and the cold, hard pellets stung Nancy's face. She pulled the hood of her parka tighter around her head.

After fifty yards or so, the snowshoes started to feel unbearably cumbersome. Nancy stopped, realizing that the extreme cold had already numbed her hands. Clumsily, she took off the snowshoes and carried them under her arm.

The storm intensified by the minute. Crosscurrents of wind drove the icy-sharp sleet against her skin, and it was hard for her to see the blue markers.

Nancy wondered if Mr. Segal had underestimated the distance to Marco's cabin. Maybe I've lost track of time, she thought. She was tempted to look at her watch, but that would mean another stop, and she felt it was better to press on.

"Keep moving. Just keep moving," she said out loud. People only freeze to death when they stay still and don't realize what's happening to them, she thought grimly. Frightened by the thought, she hastened her pace, jogging as best she could through the driving storm.

After what felt like light-years, Nancy spotted the edge of the pine forest. Through the trees, she glimpsed a lone building with lights blazing. Nancy shone her flashlight on the narrow passage between the trees.

As she got closer to the bungalow, the trees thinned, and Nancy could see the cottage a bit more clearly. If it weren't for the storm, Nancy thought, the scene would be picture-perfect: Marco's gingerbread house nestled near the edge of a forest.

The front door of the cabin was locked. Nancy trudged through the snow that had begun to drift against the house and pressed her face up against a window. Wiping away the snow that clung to the glass, she peered in. There, sprawled facedown on the living room floor, was Marco Diani, her main suspect. He was lying in a pool of blood!

Chapter

Thirteen

NANCY MOVED to the front of the cabin. With some effort, she kicked open the door and rushed inside. After darting to Marco's side, she knelt beside him, careful not to disturb the surroundings. She gingerly felt for a pulse but found none.

He was obviously dead, and from the feel of his skin, Nancy judged that someone had killed him roughly an hour before.

Nancy sprang to her feet to take stock of the room. The first thing she spotted was an iron poker, covered with blood.

The other fireplace tools were untouched. Red-hot embers still burned in the grate.

Based on the position of the body, Nancy guessed there had been a scuffle before Marco died. Marco's hair was tousled, and his arms and legs were splayed.

On the floor lay a lamp with a wooden base. Nancy hypothesized that Marco had knocked it over when he fell.

The rest of the room was in remarkably good order. Nancy checked the closet and found nothing but clothing hung carefully. A cursory search of the bathroom revealed a modest shaving kit sitting on the porcelain sink.

Reluctantly Nancy returned to the body. She didn't relish being by herself with a dead man, but it wouldn't be for long, she told herself. Slowly she turned the body just enough to remove the wallet from the breast pocket. She removed one hundred dollars in tens and twenties. A quick check of the bills with a magnifying glass indicated that they were probably the real thing: The round green Treasury seal was clearly printed, and Nancy saw tiny blue fibers in the paper.

Nancy placed the victim's wallet on the fireplace mantel. Glancing back at the body, a small, black object caught her eye. A beeper connected to Marco's belt. A thought flashed through Nancy's mind: If she pressed the button, it would display the last number that Marco had called. And that could be the important clue she'd been waiting to discover.

Nancy took a pencil from her purse, reached across Marco's body, and depressed the beeper button with the eraser end. As if by magic, seven green numbers lit up on the beeper's display. Nancy immediately memorized the phone number. Fleeing from the room, she closed the door behind her and headed for the hotel office.

The trek back was even more arduous. Halfway through the journey, the snow squalls made it so difficult to see that Nancy had to shield her face with her arm, proceeding only a foot or so before stopping to make sure she was still on the path.

Trying to keep her mind on the positive side of her investigation, Nancy focused on what she would tell George when she finally reached a telephone. One call to George, she said to herself, and a whole set of support systems would be set in motion. Help would be on the way, the River Heights Police would be notified, and Nancy's father would know that she was safe.

"Mr. Segal! Mr. Segal!" she called out when she returned to the office.

"There in a moment," a voice said as the owner appeared. "You look dreadful! I had no idea you'd be back tonight. I thought you were going to visit your friend."

"I had to come back," Nancy panted. "Something terrible's happened." Nancy's words were slurred through frozen lips. "I'm afraid I need to use the phone," she explained. "There's been a murder."

Dumbstruck, the man stared at her. Nancy reached for the phone, dialed 911, and reported the crime and location. The local police would be on the scene as soon as possible, they assured her, but given the road conditions, it could take extra time.

Without pausing, Nancy hung up and dialed seven more digits. This time, she tried the number she had stored in her memory. The phone rang twice before a machine picked up. "This is Stuart Teal," Stuart's fluid baritone announced. "I'm not available to answer my phone right now, but if you leave a message—"

So Stuart was the last person Marco had contacted! Horrified, Nancy slammed down the phone, hoping that his answering machine wouldn't record the hang-up. She would prefer to take him by surprise.

Without pausing, Nancy dialed again. It was vital that she get in touch with the River Heights police. It would be easier to talk to them herself instead of having George do it. Once she was connected, a rude officer announced that Chief McGinnis was away from the station. Nancy had no time to lose. She had to tell her story to McGinnis so that the police chief could respond to it as soon as possible. The murderer could be headed toward River Heights.

As Nancy was finishing her phone call, she heard sirens blaring and saw red lights blazing on and off on the walls of the office.

Three uniformed men and one woman poured out of a squad car. They burst in, and Nancy began recounting the events of the day, beginning with Chloe's guess about Marco's whereabouts.

When Nancy was through with her tale, the senior officer spoke. "From what you're telling us," he began, "there's one man down, a murderer on the loose, and a counterfeiter still at large," he summarized.

"Exactly," Nancy said. "And there's one more thing," she said, grabbing a piece of Koshel Cottage stationery. "If you call this number, Chief McGinnis of the River Heights Police will corroborate the whole thing." She jotted down McGinnis's number and handed it to the officer.

After finishing her statement, Nancy dialed Perfect Printing and asked for Stuart Teal. He was out for the day. Nancy's mind whirred: Stuart definitely had to be her new prime suspect. It was his number on the beeper. He had not been at work all day, and he had diverted attention from himself by using romance as a smokescreen. The pieces were falling into place. Marco could have been set up by Stuart to look like the counterfeiter.

Stuart wasn't necessarily acting on his own, Nancy reasoned. He could be in with Pamela. That would account for her spending, her hostility, and her meeting with Stuart, including the warning to keep things confidential! They might have formed a counterfeiting ring.

Nancy phoned George, who answered on the first ring. After recapping the events she said, "The situation's getting worse by the minute. There are about six inches of snow on the ground and I've got to get back. Could you do me a favor and call Chloe to tell her what's happened? Then please meet me at Stuart's house in two hours," she begged.

"Just give me her phone number and his address," George said. "Nan, I'm sorry the case is turning out this way for you. I wish it had been Marco."

"I know what you mean," Nancy said.

When Nancy hung up, she was finally ready for the journey home.

The highway was deserted; Nancy drove for six miles before seeing another car. Although slippery, the roads were passable. The snow-plow must not be far ahead, Nancy reasoned. She concentrated on the road while the facts of the case bubbled in her brain. Three of her suspects —Jason, Stuart, or Pamela—could have killed Marco. Stuart was the likeliest candidate, though. Thinking back, Nancy realized that Stuart was the one person who knew about the counterfeiting from the very beginning. Hadn't he been fairly eloquent on the topic during the plant tour that first day? The accident on the loading dock—maybe one of Stuart's employees had been driving the truck. It even could have been Stuart who was responsible for the locked steam room door at the health club. Now Nancy was almost certain Stuart had to be behind her series of "accidents." He had been on the scene each and every time. Was Jason involved as well? And what about Chloe? It would be another hour before Nancy could get more answers to her hundreds of questions.

It was past eight by the time Nancy parked her Mustang several yards down from Stuart's town house. The snow had stopped, so she could spot George hunched behind the wheel of her car on the other side of the street. George looked in both directions before she jumped from the vehicle and started jogging over to the Mustang. She scooted into the passenger seat and began talking.

"I'm so glad you got back safely, Nan," she said. "I got here half an hour ago and nothing's happened." She handed Nancy a thermos of hot cocoa. "Here," she said, "you probably need this." Nancy poured herself a cup and drank it gratefully.

Headlights glared from behind. Instinctively, Nancy ducked, pulling George down with her. They heard a car screech to a halt and a door slam. Heavy footsteps faded away. Cautiously George peeked over the dashboard. "It must have been Jason—that's his Jeep!" she exclaimed.

Nancy cast her gaze on the car. "You're right, but doesn't it look kind of strange?" she wondered out loud.

George burrowed in her handbag. She pulled out a pair of binoculars and held them up to her eyes. "The whole back end of the car is lower than the front," she reported. "And there are lots of cartons stacked in the back!" she gasped.

"What do you think? Should we go and see for ourselves what's in the boxes?" George said. "We've got to get evidence, and it may as well be now. But we'd better have an airtight plan."

Nancy agreed. She was afraid of what the consequences could be if they weren't in sync with each other.

"We can make a run for the car and get in on

the passenger side," Nancy said. "But we should have a backup in case it's locked."

"How about for plan B we run back to the car and wait for them to come out of the house?" George proposed.

"That should work," Nancy told her. "On the count of three?" she asked George with a tremor in her voice.

"One, two—" George slid out of the car and soundlessly pushed the door shut. Nancy followed. Coming around the front of the car, they glanced at each other to make sure they were both ready. After a second they bolted toward Jason's Jeep.

George grabbed the rear door of the vehicle and was overjoyed to find it unlocked. She opened the door just enough to squeeze through and crawled toward the other side to make room for Nancy. When both girls were safely inside, Nancy pulled the car door closed most of the way.

She felt her heart thudding in her chest. Just the night before she'd been in Stuart's arms, and now she was collecting evidence against him— for counterfeiting and maybe even for murder.

The girls peered cautiously over the backseat of the Jeep. "There are at least nine boxes here," George whispered. "Might as well start with the closest one." Nancy reached into her jeans pocket and drew out her key chain. Using the sharp edge of her house key, she split the taped seam.

Inside they found pile after pile of white paper, all the same rectangular size, neatly stacked. Nancy touched the top piece and hissed, "Let's see if this is what I think it is." She dipped into her pocket again and produced a dollar bill. Unfolding it, she held it up against one of the white rectangles in the box. It matched perfectly.

"Yup," she confirmed, "this is what we've been looking for: authentic currency paper! These are one-dollar bills that've been bleached out so they can be reprinted—probably as counterfeit fifties!"

Chapter

Fourteen

JUST THEN, a clatter sounded from the direction of the town house. Nancy and George scrambled out of the car, easing the door closed behind them. "Quick!" Nancy whispered. "Over here!" She shoved George behind the trunk of a pine tree. She was terrified that they'd be seen or heard.

As the two figures climbed into the Jeep, Nancy identified Jason and Stuart by their profiles.

George touched Nancy's arm when she recognized the men. Nancy held her breath; it was hard for her not to cry out.

Jason drove on as the Jeep fishtailed down the snowy street.

When the car was almost out of sight, Nancy and George took off for Nancy's Mustang. "He may be going to print them up now!" Nancy blurted out as they ran.

"Yeah," huffed George, "and with all that paper, they'll have big bucks by the time they're through."

"They need a printing press to do it. They must be headed for Perfect Printing!" Nancy deduced, driving her car with George in it.

"We'll let them get there first, then we'll follow and catch them in the act!" George said.

"That's the plan." Nancy nodded. She felt the hair on the back of her neck prickle. If their hunch was right and Stuart was involved, Pamela could be as well. They'd be outnumbered.

The front lot at Perfect Printing was ghostly, with the thick layer of snow stretched across it and no cars in sight. The girls parked a safe distance past the plant, behind a deserted shed off the main road.

They got out of the car and started slogging through the snow back toward the factory. They sneaked around to the back. Jason's Jeep was right next to the loading dock. Stuart's sedan was stationed beside it. Stuart must have left his car there that afternoon and gotten a ride home with Jason, Nancy deduced.

Walking farther around the building's perimeter, Nancy carefully tried to turn the knob to the back door of the stockroom. Finding it locked, she and George backtracked to the side of the building.

Light glowed through a bank of small-paned windows roughly eight feet above the ground. "Do you think we could make it through there?" George whispered.

"It looks like we're going to have to try," Nancy answered. "Can I have a leg up?" she asked George.

George laced the fingers of her gloved hands together. She formed a step for Nancy to hop up on. George held Nancy steady as she pushed the window open and peered in, taking in as much of the scene as she could.

The rattle of a printing press could be heard loudly and clearly. Nancy spotted the machine smack in the center of the printing room floor. Stuart stood at the front end, stacking the dollar-size piles of paper into the feeder tray. The sleeves of his white shirt were rolled up; he wore a denim apron to protect his clothing. There could be no doubt about it now: Stuart was in on the counterfeiting plot! Could he have been forced by Jason to help out? she wondered. There was only a ghost of a chance of that, she thought sadly.

"Nan, can I let you down now?" George hissed. "My hands are killing me!"

"One more sec," Nancy responded. She craned her neck in order to see the back end of the press. There stood Jason, feet apart, hands clasped behind him. He stared, mesmerized as fake money spewed from the printing press!

Nancy hopped down and described the scene to George. "This is our only chance to stop them," Nancy told her. "It's now or never! We'll go in and head them off. They're sure to want to get out of town for a while before those bills get into circulation!"

George nodded. "Come here. I'll give you a leg up. Only this time, go all the way in, and I'll follow." She hoisted Nancy up to the window once again. When Nancy was safely inside, she leaned out to give George a hand to pull her up.

The noise from the printing press camouflaged the sound of their movements. They were hidden from Jason and Stuart by a stack of paper cartons. All at once the presses stopped. Kneeling, Nancy peered around the edge of the cartons to see why.

"Hey," Jason said, raising his head. "Why'd you stop the press?" he demanded of Stuart.

"Paper jam," replied Stuart. "I'll have it under control in a minute."

"You'd better," Jason shot back, "or whatever we can't finish comes out of *your* pocket!"

"I've had enough of your attitude, man," Stuart responded, throwing his apron aside and stalking Jason. "If you weren't so greedy we wouldn't be doing this at the last minute anyway!"

"Greedy?" Jason intoned. "I'm just the same as you, pal. Don't forget we're splitting everything fifty-fifty."

Nancy caught George's eye. Stuart *was* in on the deal—it was official. George touched Nancy's arm in silent sympathy.

"I wouldn't call the deal fair exactly," Stuart said. "I never agreed to fake those ridiculous-looking bills on the copy machine. I was the one who wanted to do this right from the very beginning. I was careful not to get caught. Getting the ink from Switzerland—do you think it was easy faking the documents for that? Then you blew it all because you got greedy and copied a little pocket money."

"How did I know a few color-copied bills would get us into trouble? All I did was switch a few fake twenties for real ones in Chloe's wallet."

So that's how she got them! Nancy marveled. This guy really thinks he's got all the angles covered, she thought.

"You're just mad because you couldn't get Nancy to fall for you. If it was my job, I'd have won her over in fifteen minutes," Jason boasted.

How dare he think he could get away with trying to *make* me fall in love with him! Nancy thought. The nerve of them! Nancy shifted her weight to relieve the pressure on her aching knees. Without realizing it, she nudged the center carton several inches too far, throwing the stack of cartons out of balance. She could only watch, horrified and helpless, as they toppled to the floor, creating a thunderous, avalanchelike sound.

George gasped. Nancy, stunned, brought her hands to her face. She glimpsed Jason glowering at them.

"Nancy—no!" Stuart shouted. "It's not what you think!" he cried, bolting in her direction. Nancy grabbed George's arm and began running away from Stuart at full speed. Nancy glanced back to see that the men were gaining on them.

"The loading dock," George rasped.

"Uh-huh," Nancy grunted. Both knew it was their only way out.

"Hit the loading dock gate!" Jason shrieked to Stuart.

Nancy and George watched, terrified, as the loading dock gate inched down toward the floor to lock them in.

Nancy's lungs felt ready to explode. If they didn't reach the gate before it hit the floor . . .

Nancy glanced back to see the men gaining on them. Now they were only a few paces back. With no time to deliberate, she swung her arm out toward a shelf of ink rollers, flinging whatever she could grab onto the floor. The men stumbled and went down like bowling pins; it was impossible for them to keep their footing on the metallic cylinders.

Nancy heard Jason curse as he hit the ground. "You girls think you're so smart," he shouted angrily, "but I'll get you!"

"Please, Nancy," Stuart implored. "Stop running and I'll explain. We'll work it out—I swear!"

The voice was closer this time, maybe five feet back.

Nancy's heart pounded wildly. What if they got caught? Would Jason even hesitate before killing them?

Nancy and George were within a few feet of the loading dock when they heard the sound of metal against concrete moving toward them. Nancy whipped around to see a large black industrial barrel on its side, rolling across the floor like an oversize bowling ball. The words *DANGER* and *FLAMMABLE* flashed at her. Nancy tried to think how to dodge the deadly drum, but it was no use: The huge keg of chemicals kept coming straight at them!

Chapter

Fifteen

THERE WAS NO PLACE to go but up. When the
barrel was nearly at their feet, George yelled,
"Nancy, jump!" At the exact moment the barrel
threatened to knock them over, both girls leapt
high into the air, grabbed hold of the gate, and
clambered up it.

The drum of chemicals rolled under them and
hit the loading dock gate. The noise it created
sounded as loud as that made by a kettle drum.

Miraculously, the toxic contents remained
sealed inside.

As Nancy and George started down the gate,
they faced yet another challenge. Jason tackled
them and pulled them to the ground. He laughed
unpleasantly.

Nancy and George stayed on the ground, waiting to see what would happen next.

Jason grabbed something from his vest pocket. Nancy saw a glint of steel in the harsh fluorescent light. It was a revolver! He waved it wildly in the girls' faces. Nancy refused to let herself flinch. She knew she couldn't overpower Jason, but she felt she had a good chance of outsmarting him.

"The gun says it all, eh, girls?" He chuckled. "Stu!" he barked. "Get me some rope!"

There was no reply.

As he waited for Stuart to return, Jason marched the girls into the plant's darkroom.

"We didn't see this place on the tour," George whispered to Nancy.

"There's a lot you gals haven't seen," Jason told her. "But this ought to keep you out of trouble for a while—before you're put away *permanently,*" he threatened. He forced the girls to sit on straight-backed wooden chairs.

Stuart reappeared a minute later with black electrical cord in his hands. Slowly he began tying Nancy and George's hands behind their backs. "I never thought I'd be doing this," he said with tension in his voice.

"You don't have to be doing this," Nancy said, trying to give Stuart the idea that he could disobey Jason, who was clearly the one giving orders.

"You've got to believe me, Nancy," Stuart said. "There's a long story to this, and it's not as bad as it looks."

"I do believe you," Nancy told him, hoping he would tell her everything.

"The real story's just so different from everything I led you to believe," he said, ashamed. "The printing business has been really tough this year. We've been losing money. I've been working hard trying to get new business, but there's too much competition. There are tons of printers around Chicago.

"When Jason and I first started talking about counterfeit money, it was just a joke, a gag."

"What do you mean?" Nancy asked. She wanted to know if Stuart had become involved in the plot willingly or if Jason had egged him on.

"I never thought you'd meant it at first, Jase," Stuart said sadly, addressing his partner. "It was all fun at the beginning, how great it would be to make money the 'easy' way.

"Before I knew it, I was talking to security printers, reading articles about counterfeiters. It was almost a hobby. But all too soon it became a plan." Stuart paused and looked at Jason.

"What are you looking at me for," Jason challenged. "I didn't force you into anything."

Stuart responded gently, "I know you didn't, Jase. I got into this because I didn't want my father to think I was running his business into the ground. I started out just planning to print up some cash—two million to split, we thought. That was eight months ago." Stuart's voice was starting to crack.

"And then what happened?" Nancy prompted.

Jason cut in. "Stuart over here is such a perfectionist, he wanted every little thing to be just right," he sneered. "If we'd done it *his* way, we wouldn't be doing it for forty years. You'd think he was making a masterpiece instead of dough."

What an incredible creep this guy is, Nancy thought. He was using exactly the same tone with Stuart that he had with Marco.

"But I have to admit," Jason continued, "we were inspired! I kicked into gear with a plan that showed true genius," Jason boasted.

"You sure fooled me," Nancy said, encouraging him to tell the story. "How did you do it?" she pressed.

"We bleached out the one-dollar bills so we'd have the right paper," Jason gloated. "Then we just needed the fancy ink. Stu set that up with his Swiss contact. Those bozos actually thought we were trying to get qualified to become real currency printers—the documents we forged were that good!"

"And what about Marco?" Nancy questioned,

trying to keep them talking. Her wrists were beginning to ache; the cord was just tight enough to dig into her skin.

"Marco had the training to do a great design job. And we needed top-quality original art to print from," Stuart admitted.

"So we blackmailed him!" Jason said with an eerie sense of pride. "We told him that if he didn't help out, we'd let everyone in River Heights know he went to a juvenile school for counterfeiting. I'll bet his banking client would've *loved* that one!" He chuckled.

"How did you know about his past?" George queried, keeping her voice even.

"From Chloe, of course," Jason said. He leaned against the photo enlarger and crossed his arms, but Nancy noticed that he kept the revolver in hand, his finger poised on the trigger.

"But Chloe's not involved," Stuart said, defending her. "Chloe doesn't know anything about this whole business. And no one would've gotten hurt at all if it hadn't been for *him.*" He nodded toward Jason. "He thought it'd be convenient to just run off a few bills on a color copier. Without even asking me! And for what?" Stuart shook his head dolefully.

Sounds as if he has regrets, Nancy thought. But it still doesn't make him any less guilty, she reminded herself. As Nancy listened, she tried to work the cord over her wrists to free her hands. It was futile; the binding was just too tight.

"Tell me something else," Nancy asked. "How does Pamela fit into all this?"

"Pamela?" Stuart said, puzzled. "She's really a client. Why do you ask?"

"Her spending is out of control."

"She has nothing to do with us," Jason said vehemently. "I told you this whole thing was my idea."

"Then what did she tell you that was confidential the other day," Nancy persisted.

"Oh, that," Stuart remembered. "Pamela knows I'm aware she's in big debt. She wanted to make sure I wouldn't tell."

No wonder Pamela was nervous around Nancy and George. She was worried that the counterfeiting investigation would reveal her debt problem.

The next question was directed at Jason. "Why did you kill Marco?" Nancy asked, trying not to reveal her contempt.

Stuart said hurriedly, "Getting rid of Marco wasn't part of the original plan. Otherwise I'd never have agreed to it."

"Get real, Teal," Jason snarled, drawing a step closer to him and to the girls. "You knew from the start this was going to take guts. And, anyway, we *had* to waste the guy."

"Why?" Nancy repeated. The longer she could keep Jason talking, the better her odds of escape, she reasoned.

"Marco got too antsy," Jason answered. "He didn't want to have anything to do with us, and he didn't have the stomach for any of this. We got him to drive the truck to the loading dock that day you toured the plant. To get him to do it, we told him we were just making a delivery, and that it was no big deal. But he freaked when I chucked the carton out the back door at you guys." He pointed to Nancy and George. "What a coward," Jason snickered. "He would have opened his mouth and spilled the whole thing if I hadn't shut him up. He was about to tell you everything the night of the awards dinner—he was threatening me."

No wonder Marco had acted so strangely all the time. He must have been constantly debating whether to risk exposing his own past by turning in Jason and Stuart!

Nancy thought more about Marco's behavior. Knowing what he knew about Jason, he wouldn't have wanted to go into business with Chloe as long as Jason was in the picture. It was probably Marco who left the hang-ups on her answering machine and the note under her windshield. He had been trying to break the story to her! All of a sudden the whole thing seemed terribly tragic to

Nancy. How many times had Marco thought about telling Chloe the truth about her boyfriend?

"Maybe he was a weakling," Stuart said, turning to Jason, "but he didn't deserve to die." He faced Nancy now. "Don't blame me, please, Nancy," he said. "I didn't even know Jason was going to kill Marco to shut him up. And I really cared about you—I still d-do," he stammered.

"I believe you," she said, and she did. Stuart, she could see in hindsight, was charming but essentially weak. She felt disgusted that he'd manipulated her, but she was also satisfied that she'd been in control enough not to be totally taken in by him. After all, she had kissed him only that one time.

Sensing her friend's uneasiness, George stepped in and kept Stuart talking. "Why did you start up with Nancy in the first place?" she asked bluntly.

Stuart stared at his feet, ashamed. "Jason made me do it in the beginning. He thought that if I kept her busy, I could keep her off our trail. Nancy was too sharp for that," Stuart said.

"Bet you'll change your tune when you see the bags of dough," Jason said, cutting him off. "So why don't you quit whining? I had to ice Marco before we did the print run. He could have blown it wide open. When I called Chloe, she told me where he'd gone. Chloe's the one who tipped me off that you were on your way to Marco's. So I had Stuart here do a job on your tire."

"I knew what I was doing, Nancy. I knew how to do it so that you'd only get scared and not hurt. I was still trying to warn you away. It was the same with the sauna—I just wanted you to quit the investigation. It was the same with Marco. I warned him to stay away from Jason. He even called me this afternoon to get me to reassure him that he was safe from Jason. I really thought he was. I had no idea Jason would kill him."

Stuart was mortified. Nancy glared at him, shaking her head in disbelief. He had been deluded in thinking that no one could have gotten hurt, and he had been mistaken to believe that his intimidation would scare her away.

"If Stu had been doing his job, you wouldn't have followed at all. He was supposed to get you out of the way—for good!" Jason stepped forward and aimed the gun at Stuart.

"You're no longer useful to me, Stuart," he said, grinning crazily. "And besides, two million bucks sounds a lot better than one million! Get down on the floor, good buddy. You're about to become history!"

Chapter

Sixteen

TRAINING THE REVOLVER on Stuart's head, Jason used his free hand to wind the wire around Stuart's wrists.

"You don't want to be doing this," Stuart said frantically. "We'll work things out if you'll just put the gun down." The printer lay facedown on the floor.

"I'd like you to stick around for just a few more minutes until I'm sure I'm not having any printing problems you need to help me with," Jason said as he strode out of the dark room, leaving the door open a crack. After several minutes they heard the sound of the press start up: Jason was printing the money!

THE NANCY DREW FILES

The noise of the press was deafening. For twenty tense minutes, there was no communication among the hostages in the darkroom.

Then through the crack Nancy spied Jason stacking the finished cash in cartons. When he had packed and taped the last box, he began loading them into his Jeep. Nancy could just see the open loading dock gate.

Even after he'd finished the run, Jason kept the press running. For the racket, Nancy thought. So no one would hear us calling, as if there were anyone to hear! Still, there must be some way to escape. Her chair was up against a work table. She explored the surface with her hands. She felt something cold and sharp. Running her fingers around it, she rotated it to explore the size of the object.

It was a metal printing plate, slightly larger than a piece of paper. Its edges were razor-sharp! Cautiously Nancy worked her hands back and forth against the knifelike edge. After a full five minutes of sawing, she cut through the bonds and yanked her hands free at last!

Nancy popped up and untied George as well. She would leave Stuart where he was; she didn't trust him. Cupping her hands, she spoke directly into George's ear. "At the count of three, we'll go for Jason," Nancy said, seeing him bent over the last of the cartons. "You jump him. I'll grab the gun."

They watched him for another minute before springing into action.

George was the first to lunge. She tackled Jason at the knees, knocking him to the ground. The gun skidded across the floor. Nancy tried to snatch it, but it was too late. The gun was out of sight, underneath the printing press!

Jason was on the floor, with George holding him in a half nelson. Jason struggled frantically in an attempt to get free, but George managed to restrict his range of motion.

"The gun!" she called out to Nancy. Nancy flew to the printing press, yanking the lever to shut it down so she could get under it. She needed the weapon so she could keep control.

In the second of silence that followed, a shout rang out. "Nancy! Behind you!" Stuart yelped. Stuart's hands and feet were still tied, but he'd managed to get himself to a seated position to warn Nancy.

Jason flew at Nancy, pushing her off balance. She fell back into a massive metal shelf, unleashing boxes that spilled shredded paper like snow.

Nancy couldn't see anything; the air was thick with confetti. But she heard the clatter of the press being moved. Jason was going for the gun!

Nancy could see clearly now as Jason reached up, gun in hand, and swung his arm around George's neck. Her head was in the crook of his elbow; he held it there in a viselike grip.

"Hold on, George," Nancy called.

George couldn't speak, but her eyes expressed her terror.

"I guess I'll have to take her with me," Jason snarled, pointing the weapon at George's temple. "So I wouldn't try anything stupid if I were you, Ms. Hotshot Detective, or you'll be going to your friend's funeral!" He grabbed the remains of the cord and bound George's hands once again.

Nancy watched, frozen, as Jason jabbed the button to open the loading dock door. As soon as the space was wide enough, he pushed George out, holding her arm to keep her from escaping.

Jason moved through the door, too. In the split second that his back was turned, Nancy acted. She flung herself at him, landing a karate chop on the back of his neck. In her left hand she wielded a heavy metal printing roller like a baseball bat. She followed up the chop with a forceful wallop to his gut.

"Urhg," Jason grunted, lurching to the floor. George pulled loose from his grip and hopped back inside as Nancy dropped the roller and yanked the gun from Jason's hand. She trained the gun on Jason, who was climbing to his feet.

"Okay, just calm down," Jason spat out.

"I *am* perfectly calm," Nancy told him without flinching. "Don't move an inch," she said with steel in her voice.

"Get real," Jason said. "You wouldn't shoot me." He was testing her.

"Try me," Nancy said simply, and Jason stood stock-still.

George led Jason into the darkroom.

Nancy motioned for Stuart and Jason to sit in the same chairs in which they had held the girls captive. "I was willing to give up. I wanted Jason to turn himself in, and I was willing to call off the counterfeiting operation from the time you arrived here today," Stuart went on.

"Is that why you tied us up?" Nancy asked pointedly.

"I had to, or Jason would've killed me," Stuart asserted.

"All I can say is I hope that both of you are fond of enclosed spaces—and of each other," Nancy said. "Because you're going to be spending a lot of Christmases together behind bars!"

The River Heights Mall buzzed with people the next day, the last shopping day before Christmas. Nancy, George, and Bess sat at a table in the food court sipping mulled cider, talking over the whirlwind week now behind them.

"It probably wouldn't have taken so long if I hadn't thought Marco was guilty," George worried.

"Forget it, George," Nancy reassured her friend. "How could you have known Marco was being blackmailed? It really looked like he was doing the counterfeiting all along."

"I feel really bad for Chloe," George told her friends. "She looked wrecked this morning when we explained what the deal was."

"Poor thing," said Bess. "Her best friend's dead and her boyfriend's a crook. That's some Christmas present! What's she going to do?"

"She said she'd be spending the holidays with her family in Chicago," Nancy answered. "And Chloe's no fool. She was starting to suspect there was something going on with Jason. It's Marco she's most upset about."

"Speaking of boyfriends," George said, "what's the story with Kyle?"

Bess sniffled. "The romance is definitely over," she reported. "We were glad to see each other and everything, but we can't have a long-distance relationship."

"Don't worry, Bess, you'll meet someone else," Nancy reassured her. "Weren't there any cute guys out there?" she asked.

Bess brightened. "Lots," she said. "And all of

the law students were adorable! I can't wait to go to college so I can graduate and start law school!"

Nancy and George laughed.

The mood turned more serious. "Did you get your feelings hurt over Stuart?" George quietly asked Nancy.

"I did like him," Nancy admitted. "He was so sophisticated, but I have tonight to look forward to—Ned's coming home. Ned!" she gasped. The stores were closing early and she still didn't have his present! "I've got to get him something fabulous—and fast!" she groaned.

"Be cool, Nan," said George, "I've got the perfect gift. Just give Ned a beeper. That way, the two of you will never be out of touch again!"

Nancy's next case:

For Nancy and Ned, a week alone together in Washington State is a dream come true: days rushing down the ski slopes, evenings cuddling by the fire. But at the last moment, their vacation plans take a chilling turn. An invitation to scale majestic Mount Rainier draws them to the edge of an icy and potentially lethal precipice of mystery and danger! Kara and Alex Wheeler, owners of the Alpine Adventures guide service, have been victimized by a campaign of terror—anonymous threats, midnight break-ins, sabotaged equipment. But to get to the bottom of the case, Nancy must go to the top of Mount Rainier: steep, rugged, isolated . . . the perfect setting for a cliffhanger and a deadly surprise . . . in *Heart of Ice,* Case #103 in The Nancy Drew Files™.